Festival of Crime

Festival of Crime

Nineteen Tales of
Murder and Suspense by
Twin Cities Sisters in Crime

edited by

Christine Husom,
Mickie Turk, and
Michael Allan Mallory

NODIN PRESS

Acknowledgments:
The stories in FESTIVAL OF CRIME take place at fairs, festivals, and special events in Minnesota. Set in different regions of the state, some use the actual festival name while others rely on a stand in.

This anthology is a product of members of Twin Cities Sisters in Crime. Sisters in Crime is a national organization founded to promote the professional development of women crime writers and to help them achieve equality in the industry. Membership is open to both women and men, as evidenced by the stories in this collection.

The editors—Christine Husom, Mickie Turk, and Michael Allan Mallory—wish to thank all the writers who submitted stories. Our special thanks to Norton Stillman and John Toren at Nodin Press, and to Dan Bernier, a Sisters in Crime brother, for his invaluable assistance.

Design: John Toren
cover photo © Stephanie Swartz | Dreamstime.com

Library of Congress Cataloging-in-Publication Data

Festival of crime : nineteen tales of murder and suspense by Twin Cities Sisters in Crime / edited by Christine Husom, Mickie Turk, and Michael Allan Mallory.
pages cm
ISBN 978-1-935666-64-6
1. Detective and mystery stories, American--Minnesota. 2. Festivals--Minnesota--Fiction. 3. Minnesota--Fiction. I. Husom, Christine, editor of compilation. II. Turk, Mickie, editor of compilation. III. Mallory, Michael Allan, editor of compilation.
PS374.D4F47 2014
813'.08720832776--dc23

2014005848

Nodin Press
5114 Cedar Lake Road,
Minneapolis, MN 55416

Contents

Foreword

What do a dogsled race, a wooden boat show, a raptor release, a Winter Carnival, and a gay pride parade have in common? Within the pages of this collection at least, the answer is: Murder!

These nineteen authors dive (with a vengeance, you might say) into every imaginable kind of celebration—art fairs and traveling carnivals, colorful fiestas, and small-town crazy days. They take us on roller-coaster rides that offer thrills and chills, exploring the dark underbelly of small town and big city life, where love and money provide familiar motives for murder, and where the past has a habit of rising up to haunt evildoers.

There is something quintessentially Minnesotan about every one of these stories—they revel in our local love of celebrations, whatever the season. Why, just sitting in your chair reading you can see your breath while mushing with the dogsled teams or carving shimmering blocks of solid ice in the dead of winter. Enjoy the burgeoning spring high above the Mississippi at Cinco de Mayo, and soak up the summer heat as you listen to the lazy sound of grasshoppers in dusty late July cornfields. Take in the sights and smells of the carnival midway, the air redolent with machine oil and mini-donuts. Feel the nip in the air at Oktoberfest or the annual Scarecrow contest at the harvest fair.

I recommend reading slowly to really savor the rich stew of characters who inhabit these stories, from psychopaths and cagey con men, to twisted cops and shrewd amateur sleuths.

Thanks to Twin Cities Sisters in Crime for giving us so much to celebrate—as if we needed an excuse!

– Erin Hart, author of *The Book of Killowen*,
number 4 in the Nora Gavin/Cormac Maguire mystery series

Sawbill Checkpoint

Michael Allan Mallory

Craig Burgess grimaced against a frigid January wind that was determined to turn him into a six-foot icicle. Feet swathed in Alpine mukluks stamped the hard pack. Not from cold. Nerves. He scanned the snow-covered trail that cut through the pine forest like a white scar, bleak and unpromising. "Not much out here, Norm," he said, trying to veil his apprehension. Mitch was overdue, should have been in the first group of mushers. It had been forty minutes since the eighth sled dog team pulled into Sawbill—Jerry Kleinschmidt's team. No way would Mitch have let Kleinschmidt get ahead of him. Not if he was still in the race.

Norm, who had been crouching to adjust a propane tank, hauled himself to his feet with an effort and snuggled deeper into his parka as the metal cooker worked slowly to a boil. The dogs would be hungry when they got in. "Something's not right. Mitch shoulda been here by now." His bearded face—usually full of good cheer and easy laughter—looked back with concern. For Norm, a man so innately optimistic he could find a silver lining in even the blackest cloud, that was definitely out of character. Few things ever fazed him. Strong, ruggedly built, dependable to the max, if he'd been a Siberian Husky he'd be a wheeler, one of the dogs closest to the sled. The anchor. Craig relied on Norm's steadfastness and wished he had better news for his teammate; yet all either man could do was give the other a grim nod and pray their leader was merely delayed and not hurt.

It didn't help that Sawbill was a wilderness checkpoint. Isolated. While not as grueling in distance as the famed Iditarod, the Dan Elkhorn Sled Dog Marathon was the longest such race in the lower forty-eight states, and considered among the toughest for its rugged, hilly terrain, sharp inclines, and steep drops—an endurance challenge all its own. A harsh bump at speed could send a musher flying off narrow sled runners, only to be left behind by a dog team enthralled by the run and suddenly unburdened by the weight of their driver, who now was left to fend for himself within the wilds of Superior National Forest in bitter January weather.

The hard snap of canvas stole Craig's attention. The Dan Elkhorn race banner billowed above the checkpoint roadway like a sail in the wind. Nearby dog teams rested on freshly laid straw while their handlers tended to them. Craig stamped his feet in the snow again. More nervous energy. If Mitch got in before nightfall he'd be okay. Still a few hours left till then, but the sun was already on the downward swing of its low winter arc.

"Sled!" a spectator shouted from the snow fence. Hundreds of onlookers had braved the cold to stand on either side of the raceway. Hoots and cheers encouraged the approaching team.

Craig whirled about, eyes fixed on the trail. He could just make out a sled, an undulating string of dogs and pounding orange paws. His heart leapt. *Their* dogs wore orange booties. "Norm, get your ass in gear. It's Mitch!"

Yet even as the words tumbled out he realized something was wrong. It took only a few seconds to see what it was. The sled had no driver. Mitch Travers wasn't there. The dogs were running by themselves.

A snowball-size knot twisted in Craig's belly. "We got a problem, Norm. Get help. We need a stop line!"

Craig ran for the checkpoint line. Bulky winter clothing made each stride feel as if he were dragging an anvil. With no time to waste, Craig ran by the startled checker—poised with his clipboard and watch—and hurried across the snowpack toward the oncoming dogs. Cheers from the crowd nearly drowned out the sound of his pounding heart and labored breathing. The paws of fourteen charged-up hounds thundered across the wooden footbridge. Craig skidded to a halt and calculated the distance and timing, then started back on a parallel path with the team. Could he do it? Only one shot at this, he knew, like jumping on a runaway locomotive. The dogs raced past him as he angled toward the sled. His eyes locked onto the all-too-rapidly approaching handlebar. He lunged and grabbed for dear life. Arctic thermal mitts struggled to hang on. For an instant Craig thought he'd fall, yet his grip held. With his last remaining strength he hoisted his feet onto the runners.

He was on.

"Easy!" he called, feeling the sled rumble under him. "Easy!"

There were no reins on a dog sled; the team obeyed vocal commands—when they had a mind to, though in the frenzy of a run they might not. Craig's boot pressed hard on the center brake. The metal plate bit into the hard pack. "Whoa!" Ranger and Oska, the lead dogs, the smartest and most driven, didn't seem to care; they were on a mission. The sled slowed, but not quickly enough. The checker barely jumped out of the way in time. "Whoa!" Craig jammed down the brake and the sled shuddered into deceleration. Still not fast enough; the stop line was coming up too fast, the people on it braced for impact, so for good measure Craig yanked the snow hook from its holster and threw it down. The polyethylene line paid out and snapped taut as twin metal bear claws dug into the snow, jerking the dogs to a full stop just in time. Handlers immediately swarmed the dog team with praise, lavished on each animal with ample petting. Exhausted, Craig huffed out jets of white vapor and caught his breath for a moment before helping Norm unfasten the tug line from Ranger's X-harness.

Norm looked over anxiously. "What happened to Mitch?"

"I don't know. We'll get to that. First the dogs."

Caring for the dogs was their first priority, callous as that seemed. Tired dogs had to be unbuckled from the tug line, their paws inspected by veterinary volunteers and then fed. For a few minutes Mitch had to wait, agonizing as it was. Even if they wanted to search for him, where on the thirty miles between Sawbill and Devil Track would they look? For all Craig knew Mitch was fine. Perhaps he had taken a spill and was getting a lift from another musher. As soon as the initial tasks were completed and Craig could delegate the handling of the dogs, he'd work out a plan with race officials. Until then, he prayed for good news.

That hope was crushed ten minutes later when Karen Fuller's team rumbled across the Temperance River footbridge. Her sled flew into the checkpoint and slammed to a stop in a spray of snow. She ignored the checker as he approached with the sign-in clipboard. Her tear-marked face released the words she'd kept to herself for the last heartbreaking miles.

"Mitch Travers is dead. Somebody shot him."

❀

Deputy Sheriff Marge Erdahl had assessed the situation quickly after the drive from Tofte and was ready to take charge. She'd run into enough people who hadn't taken her seriously as a peace officer because of her looks or gender, not only men but women as well. Experience had taught her to come into a new situation with her guns drawn, so to speak, in order to forestall any opposition. While on the job her appealing face and winsome eyes were strictly business, and her shapely figure was tamed beneath a winter uniform.

Not one to waste time on pleasantries, especially with a biting wind gnawing at her, Erdahl fastened her resolute eyes on Karen Fuller and said, "How'd you find Mr. Travers' body?" Karen looked back with a face dulled by sadness and the anguish of her grim discovery. Hair the color of red copper protruded beneath a black wool stocking cap. "I'd just rounded Pike Lake," she managed with effort, forcing herself to remember that which she cared not to remember. "There are some sharp turns that straighten out into a long stretch before the trail crosses Murmur Creek Road. That's where I found Mitch, lying on his back in the snow. I stopped my team to see if I could help, but,"—she swallowed hard—"he had only seconds left."

Deputy Erdahl, who'd been paying close attention to Karen's narrative, leaned forward with new interest. "Pardon? Did you just say Travers was still alive when you found him?"

"Yeah."

"What kind of shape was he in?"

"Really bad. When I first saw him I thought he was dead. When I touched him and he stirred, I nearly jumped out of my skin. He was hanging on by a thread. Like I said, only seconds left."

"Could he talk?"

"Not right away. He was pretty out of it. I saw the blood, the gunshot wound, and wondered if I should get him on my sled and bring him back. Before I could do it, he passed." Karen's eyes shuttered closed. "He was a good guy," she added in a voice of remembrance.

"You knew him well?"

Karen shrugged. "We dated for a while last fall."

"You went out with him?" The deputy's contoured eyebrows arched. "Were you lovers?"

Karen was taken aback by the directness of the question. "Gee, Deputy, that's kind of a personal question."

"Sorry, Ms. Fuller, but you can't get a more personal crime than murder."

She looked back in some astonishment. "You think I killed Mitch?"

"Look, I'm just gathering information. But I will say it is interesting that you had a relationship with Mr. Travers, an intimate relationship from the sound of it. You're also the one who found his body. Quite a coincidence."

A flash of annoyance. "That's all it is, coincidence."

"And yet the fact remains," said the deputy in an undertone. "Too bad Mr. Travers didn't live long enough to tell you what happened to him."

"Oh, but he did."

"*Excuse me?*" Deputy Erdahl moved back half a step. For the first time since arriving on the scene the steely-eyed officer was rattled. "What did he say?"

Karen cast her mind back. "Mitch was barely there. His eyes fluttered open as I spoke to him; he struggled to form words. It was difficult. Finally he forced out a name."

"A name?"

"Emily."

The deputy blinked. "Emily," she puzzled. "That's what he said? Emily?"

"Yes. I asked him to repeat it. Mitch barely got the name out the second time before he died, but the name was Emily. I'm positive. She's the one you want."

Dogs barking at the prospect of food, the clank of metal pots, and the chatter of people filled the next few seconds as Deputy Erdahl reflected on Karen's story. "That was lucky," she finally said with an enigmatic smile that stretched the fine lines of her mouth. "I mean that you got there in time to hear that."

Karen gave a half-hearted shrug. "I guess."

"Does the name mean anything to you?"

"Emily? No, sorry."

"You knew Mr. Travers. Any of his friends or acquaintances go by that name?"

"None I remember. But he knew a lot of people."

"Maybe someone associated with the race?"

"I suppose. None of the mushers, though. There are three female mushers in the race and I've met the other two."

"I see. How about you, Mr. Burgess?'

Craig had only been half-following the conversation, fading in and out of his own reverie. The three of them stood in a small clearing away from the main action amid a clump of red pines and birch saplings, which offered a measure of privacy. Craig wasn't sure how he felt as different emotions tugged at him. Sadness. Numbing disbelief over Mitch's death. Regret at the argument they'd had at the start of the race three days ago. It was a silly squabble, nothing really. Just tension fueled by the frigid weather and pre-race jitters. They'd smoothed things over before the race began but the moment wore heavily on Craig who hoped that hadn't been Mitch's last memory of him.

"Mr. Burgess?"

Deputy Erdahl's voice pulled him back to the present moment. "Oh, sorry," he said, embarrassed. "What was the question?"

"Does the name Emily mean anything to you?"

"Uh, no."

"Did Mr. Travers know anyone by that name?"

"I can't say. Mitch knew a lot of women. The man was good looking, smart, great personality. Women loved him, like bees to a flower." Craig glanced awkwardly toward Karen, realizing his comment might have been in poor taste. "Not that Mitch talked about all the women he went out with," he backpedaled, "and sometimes I just tuned him out. A guy can only listen to so many—"

Craig stopped as if struck by a blow. He squinted toward the snow-capped pines as the ghost of an old conversation whispered into his awareness.

"Mr. Burgess?" the deputy coaxed.

His jaw dropped at a realization. "There *was* an Emily."

"Oh?"

"This was, like, two months ago. Mitch mentioned her once, maybe twice. I totally forgot until a second ago. I didn't ask him for details. Like I said, getting the lowdown on another man's love life, particularly one as active as Mitch's, gets old when you're not in the same league. But I do recall him sounding frustrated with one particular lady friend, this Emily. Something about her being too clingy." Craig pounded mittened fists against his skull. "Dang, I know there's more. What is it?"

"No rush, Mr. Burgess; we'll have time for that later." The deputy pushed back the sleeve of her coat to check the time. "Right now we need to recover the body. Ms. Fuller, do you think you could find it again?"

"Me?" Karen made a face. "Sawbill's only a rest stop. I'm in a race!"

The deputy's unsympathetic eyes narrowed. Karen Fuller was about to get a special delivery parcel of bad news dropped on her doorstep. "Ms. Fuller, may I remind you that a man has died? As it turns out, someone you knew. You're the last person who saw Mr. Travers alive. You know where the body is. Sorry to break it to you but you're done with the race."

Hazel eyes flashed with heat then faded. It took longer for clenched shoulders to ease beneath Karen's Yukon anorak. "I'm sorry, of course I'll help. It's just so frustrating to have spent all those months training only to—" She caught herself going off on a tangent and dismissed the thought with a deep purging breath of white vapor. "That's not important now. Bringing Mitch back is."

"Good." The deputy signaled for them to walk with her. The snow crunched beneath their boots as they moved beyond a stand of spruce trees toward Six Hundred Road where the deputy's white SUV was parked in a line of vehicles. "Ms. Fuller, you said the body was near Murmur Creek Road."

"Right, we can park there. It's a short hike the rest of the way, less than two hundred yards."

"After we've secured Mr. Travers' remains, I'll need official statements from both of you."

Karen lowered her chin till it nearly touched her chest. A heartfelt sigh followed.

"You okay?" Craig asked.

"I can't forget those last moments," she said softly. "No one's ever died in my arms before."

He was taken by the tenderness in her voice. "You still cared for Mitch, didn't you?"

"Yes," she confessed, "I did. You said it yourself, Mitch was a great guy; he made you feel special. But he wasn't one to settle down with any one woman. It took me a while to figure that out. That's why I broke up with him"—a whimsical snort—"before I got sucked into the Mitchsand."

"Mitchsand?" Deputy Erdahl furrowed her brow.

"A nickname. Mitch was always giving people nicknames. He called me Red 'cause of my hair. Guess I picked up the habit from him.

Mitchsand is how I described being around him. Y'know, like quicksand. Maybe a better analogy is a walleye mesmerized by a shiny lure; you don't realize you're being reeled in until it's too late. You know how some men are, Deputy."

Erdahl quirked an eyebrow. "All too well, I'm afraid. Sometimes a gal just has to take matters into her own hands."

Sensible answer, Craig thought, although delivered rather quickly and with a sort of ruthless pragmatism that made him glad he wasn't dating the deputy, a woman who clearly was not to be trifled with. Which stirred up more old cobwebs in his mind.

"Was there something else, Mr. Burgess?"

Craig had fallen back a step. "I remember Mitch said this woman was kind of a control freak. That's why he ended it, but even afterward she wouldn't let go, not at first. It was an ugly breakup." He shook his head. "I guess that's not too helpful, Deputy."

"You never know, Mr. Burgess, you never know."

One last thing continued to bother him. "Emily. What is it about that name?"

Erdahl said nothing, instead directed her gaze toward the sky where a heavy snow had begun to fall from clouds like overstuffed gray pillows. In a few hours those downy flakes would obscure the crime scene and anything around it. Like footprints. Tire tracks.

When they reached her SUV the deputy paused and gestured for the others to wait. "Give me a second to clean out the back." She lifted the rear hatch and surreptitiously moved a blanket to cover her rifle case. Then Margery Louise Erdahl turned over an old sweatshirt to conceal the initials—her initials—embossed across the front.

Delusions

Susan Hastings

Major Spencer shook her head. "The stalker followed you halfway around the world. He's military, probably Army, and there is every reason to believe he will follow you again. You have to assume he knows who your mother is and that Carol is a good friend." She leaned forward in her chair. "You can tell no one where you're going."

Ann Cantrell turned her head and stared out at the woods surrounding the Fayetteville VA Medical Center. She'd started seeing Major Spencer for treatment after her convoy hit that last IED. In the chaos of Jalalabad's streets, with snipers lurking above and bombs lining the road, she'd started feeling watched. Followed. Like she'd felt at Fort McClellan.

She'd convinced herself that PTSD was responsible, that it was impossible the stalker followed her to Afghanistan. Then Lieutenant Danbury's body had been found, a bullet to the head, hands and feet bound, knots tied in the too-familiar pattern.

She stood and faced Spencer. "You're right, ma'am. I won't tell anyone."

❀

Ann lugged easel, paints, and canvas down the hill to the big elm overlooking a pond in the middle of Swede Hollow Park. Frogs sang in the muddy margins and a pair of swallows circled and swooped through the air. She'd arrived early for the annual Art in the Hollow festival, determined to get her favorite painting spot. The morning was perfect—cool June breezes kept the bugs under control and the sun sparkled on the water.

The frogs' song stopped abruptly as she fought with the legs of her old easel, afraid she'd snap the too-dry wood. She coerced the last piece in place and smiled as the frogs forgave the disturbance with another chorus.

After she'd left Fayetteville, she went to Washington, the state of her birth, to change her name. Given her history, the judge agreed to seal her records. She'd called her mother one last time, and with a new name, birth certificate and driver's license in hand, she'd moved to Minnesota. Swede Hollow Park had become her refuge; nestled in a hidden ravine, it was an oasis of calm below St. Paul's busy Dayton's Bluff neighborhood.

Brush in hand, she considered the scene in front of her. She'd been experimenting with different undertones trying to capture the light and subtle motion that drew her to this spot. First a brilliant royal blue spread across the canvas, then a canary-yellow wash. The rough details of the scene came next in rich browns and multiple shades of green.

Music drifted down with the first of the festivalgoers. She heard children laughing and a couple discussing the wildflowers in the field behind her.

"Captain Cantrell?"

The frogs' song cut off and Ann froze. She hadn't been addressed as captain since she'd left Major Spencer's office. Her heart pounded in her chest as she turned on her portable stool to see Sergeant David Brown smiling down at her. She barely registered the young woman whose hand he held.

She stood. "Sergeant." She didn't know what to say. The questions racing through her mind—*how did you find me? what are you doing here?*—sounded too full of fear. "How are you?"

"Doing well, ma'am. I didn't expect to see anyone I knew in the park." He laughed, then pulled the woman closer. "Honey, this is my CO from Jalalabad. My fiancé, Cheryl," he said to Ann.

She managed to smile and shake Cheryl's hand.

Brown motioned to her canvas. "So you're one of the artists." He slipped his arm around Cheryl. "She painted the most amazing scenes in Jalalabad—captured both its beauty and its horror. Did you bring any here?"

"No." Ann had put the canvases in storage. Even after months of therapy, she'd struggled to control her response to thunder and firecrackers, and avoided potential triggers, including her paintings. "I may sell what I paint today."

After the murder in Jalalabad, she'd had to consider Brown as the stalker. Before she deployed, he'd been in her company at Fort McClellan. He'd been a little too friendly one night at a bar, and she'd had to put him in his place in front of his buddies. He'd apologized the next day and was professional in the months that followed. But he was one of only a handful of people who had been stationed in both places with her.

A week later her boyfriend had been bound, hands and feet tied with an intricate pattern of knots, shot in the head and dumped in the alley behind his apartment. That night she received the first letter.

He didn't deserve you. I'll always be there for you.

In the months that followed, two soldiers in her company and the bag boy at the commissary were murdered. All shot, all bound with the intricate knot work. All followed by letters.

I loved our time together on Wednesday. Why did you ruin it by talking to that stupid prick at the commissary? Why don't you understand? I am the only friend you need.

Brown smiled, bringing Ann's attention back to the park, to him and the danger he represented. "We should keep going and let you get back to your work. It's good to see you, Captain."

Ann watched them stroll down the path, then sank back onto the stool. She picked up her brush and loaded it with paint, but her hand was shaking so badly it dropped back to the palette. Memories assaulted her—bombed out buildings, broken bodies scattered like matchsticks, the sensation of being watched.

She struggled to hear the frogs' song instead of explosions, to smell wet earth and pine instead of dust and blood and fear. She looked over her shoulder, sure someone was watching, waiting. Her breathing grew shallow and quick, her pulse raced.

She jammed paints and canvas into her backpack, uncaring that colors smeared together and stained the bag. She couldn't remember how to fold the easel, her panic rising as she pushed and pulled the unyielding legs. It finally gave way and slipped into place. She stuffed it into the pack and hurried toward the exit.

A sharp report sounded a hundred meters in front of her followed by a sickening sensation like she'd stepped out of reality. She stumbled and dropped to her knees.

She crouched in the dusty street, gripped her rifle and ran, hunched low, toward a stand of rubble that offered a bit of protection. "Peterson," she yelled. "Peterson can you hear me?"

The private didn't respond. She eased up and searched for him beyond the debris, but the harsh sun glared in her eyes and she couldn't make out his shape along the road. She counted to three, then pushed up and rushed down the street in a crazy zigzag pattern to the corner of a building. "Peterson, respond!"

Nothing. She risked a glance around the side of the building and saw a stone bridge, its double arches casting shadows along the road. The sniper could be anywhere along the bridge, but no movement betrayed his location.

She grabbed her radio. "Troops in contact. Bravo squad pinned down ten meters south of the double arched bridge. Need assistance." She waited for a response, but there was nothing. No static, no response. No help coming.

Time shifted, stretched, shifted again.

She didn't know how long she'd hidden behind the rubble. "Peterson! Report!" Where was he? She risked a look toward the bridge. Another report and a bullet hit the concrete a few inches from her head. She hunkered down, waited.

All was quiet except for a robin and the frogs.

She scuttled down the line of rubble. The road was abandoned, the dust settling. Then she saw a woman running toward the bridge.

Ann blinked. Was that Sergeant Brown's fiancé? What was she doing in Jalalabad? Ann shook her head, trying to clear it, trying to make sense of where she was, what she was seeing. Then Cheryl screamed and Ann raced toward her.

She grabbed Cheryl's arm. "We've got to get out of here."

Cheryl yanked away. "No. You have to help me get David out of the water."

"David?" Ann looked at the man lying in the shallow ditch beside the path. Not Peterson. The breeze rustled the cattails that partially hid his body. Not Jalalabad. She was reaching for him when she saw the bullet hole in his head and a few intricate knots binding his wrists. A scrap of paper was tucked between his hands, her name scribbled across the top.

"No." She stepped back. "It can't be happening again."

"God, I should have stayed with him," Cheryl sobbed, pushing through the reeds trying to pull him out of the ditch. "Help me!" she screamed at Ann.

Shaking, Ann took Cheryl's arm gently and pulled her away from the body. "We have to leave him there. We have to call the police."

"But he's hurt."

Ann pulled her down the path, away from the bridge. "He's gone, Cheryl. I'm so sorry. David's already gone."

A shiver raced up her spine. She was being watched.

She scanned the path, the bridge, the ridge of trees. There were too many places to hide. How had he found her?

She pulled her phone from the backpack, amazed she'd held onto it. She dialed 911, green paint smearing across the screen. "I'm sorry, sergeant," she whispered.

✿

Ann leaned against the elm. The frogs were singing again, happy to be separated from the noisy crowd by the police barricade that protected the crime scene.

St. Paul police had arrived within minutes of her call. They'd taken her statement, but the flashbacks made it difficult for her to separate memories and hallucinations. She hadn't told them about the note, but had kept it to read again.

I'm so relieved I found you. But you insult me by talking to these people who don't deserve your friendship. You force me to kill them. Does David's fiancé know that she has you to blame for his death?

When the detective arrived, she told him about the other murders, the letters, the PTSD. She told him this was different—not as many knots at the wrist, none at the ankles—but it was the same killer. She gave him the note and accepted his anger for tampering with evidence.

Ann closed her eyes. Her nerves jumped at the slightest unexpected sound and her brain superimposed dust, ruined buildings, and the smell of gunpowder over the green coolness of the park.

The only way back to her car was through the fair and the crowds.

She drew a shaky breath, then pushed away from the tree and trudged up the hill. She'd passed the police barricade and a jeweler's booth before a laughing child bumped into her as he ran to a woman engrossed in a pot-throwing demonstration.

Ann glanced up and saw a familiar face in the crowd. She stumbled to a halt, gripping her backpack protectively in front of her. Was that really Carol? Ann hadn't seen Carol since she'd left Jalalabad. They'd been friends since basic training, and they'd kept in touch until the day Ann walked out of Major Spencer's office. She scanned the crowd, but her friend wasn't among the people strolling from booth to booth.

A balloon popped and *she ducked, searching the high ground for snipers.* An elderly couple skirted her, staring, as she crouched in the middle of the path. It was paved and smelled of asphalt, not dirt and dust. She blinked rapidly and stood, trying to focus on the spinning mound of potter's clay.

She had to get to her car. She wanted to run, but the crowds pressed against her, forcing her to adopt their strolling gait. *She gripped her rifle, moving through the market square, ignoring the stares and whispers of the women draped head to foot in black. Sweat soaked her uniform. Rumors of an attack on the market had swirled for days; any of these women could be concealing an undergarment of explosives.*

There she was again. "Carol?" Ann called. The market vanished and she shook her head. She wasn't in Jalalabad and Carol shouldn't be in St. Paul. She searched the faces in front of her trying to find the woman who looked so much like her friend. Where did she go?

Ann slung the backpack over one shoulder and rounded a curve in the path where a reggae band's steel drums rang through the chatter and laughter, the rhythm and beat riding her taut nerves and dancing in her shallow, sharp breaths. Against a rock wall a puppet theater, gaudy with primary colors, balloons, and banners, entertained children and parents sprawled in a patch of grass. Voices magnified and blurred, melding with the music and laughter and screeching planes overhead.

It was too bright, too loud, too much. How did she ever imagine she could make it through a crowd? The tunnel leading out of the park and up to the street was less than ten meters away, but she was paralyzed, unable to push against the meandering stream of fairgoers.

A strong hand gripped her arm and pulled her up the path. *Ann slammed her combat boot down on top of the insurgent's foot, then twisted and punched upward aiming for the center of a face she knew.*

Carol caught her hand and squeezed a pressure point in her wrist that sent pain shooting up her arm. "Don't fight me, Ann."

The park came back in focus with the pain. How was it possible that Carol was in St. Paul? Today, when Sergeant Brown was killed? Disoriented, she didn't fight the tug on her arm as Carol worked a path through the crowd, afraid of the thoughts forming in her head. "Are you real?"

Please, god, let her be part of the hallucination. But Carol was in jeans, a T-shirt, and a lightweight jacket, and Ann no longer wore combat boots.

Carol laughed harshly. "You'd like that, wouldn't you? You'd like to blink me away, forget you were my friend."

Ann looked around, desperately hoping to see someone else she knew, someone to help her. "Is your family here with you? Are you on vacation?"

Carol scowled. "I don't have a family now. Jake left me and has the kids." A muscle twitched in her jaw. "Why didn't you write? Let me know where you were?"

"I had to leave before—" Ann stumbled over the words. "I needed to get away from everything."

Carol's lips were a tight, straight line. "Including me. I *needed* you, Ann. The divorce was hard, losing the kids was worse. You abandoned me."

Anger surged through Ann. "You killed them."

Carol stared at her, emotionless. "Yes."

The tunnel loomed hollow and empty as they entered it. Carol was going to kill her. For a second Ann panicked, then forced herself to relax. She faked a stumble, pulling Carol off balance, then rushed her, ramming her into the wall. She grabbed a handful of Carol's short hair and bashed her head against the concrete once, twice. Three times.

Carol swung her fist and struck Ann's ear, then pushed her hard. Ann's foot caught in a crack in the asphalt and she stumbled back, dropping her backpack. Before she could regain her balance, Carol pulled a gun out of her pocket and fired. The bullet grazed Ann's arm and knocked her on her butt. She landed on the backpack and felt a leg crack off the easel.

"Stay put," Carol snapped as Ann started to rise. Carol touched the back of her head and winced. Blood seeped down her neck, staining her jacket and shirt.

Ann sat up slowly, easing off the backpack and sliding against the tunnel wall. The anger she'd felt moments before had died down to a slow burn. "How did you find me?"

Carol shrugged. "When you disappeared, it wasn't hard to figure out you'd changed your name, and even easier to track down the documentation." She reached into a back pocket and pulled out a length of nylon rope. "Stand up and turn around."

Ann ignored the command. "The records were sealed."

"People are easy to bribe." She aimed the gun at Ann's head. "Stand up and turn around."

"But why?" Ann shook her head. "Why did you kill all those people?"

"Because they were taking you from me."

"But you had your husband, your children. We would have never been lovers."

"Lovers!" Carol looked shocked. "I'm not gay. I didn't want you to be my lover. I wanted you to be my friend."

"We *were* friends. You didn't have to kill them to be my friend."

"They took you away from me." She reached down and pulled Ann to her feet. "When you were with them, even for a few minutes, you weren't with me. You were *my* friend. *Mine.* No one else had any right to you."

"You don't own me!" Ann screamed as she grabbed Carol's gun hand, bending her fist back and down. Carol pulled the trigger and a bullet ricocheted off the wall, scattering shards of concrete.

Ann twisted her foot between Carol's legs and pulled. Carol went down with Ann on top of her, and they crashed onto the backpack. Ann slammed her fist into Carol's throat, then rolled, pinning Carol's gun arm under her. Ann wrested the gun from her grip, then scrambled to her feet and took aim. But it wasn't necessary. The jagged edge of the easel's broken leg protruded from Carol's chest.

Ann heard sirens screaming on the street above the tunnel and slumped against the wall. Her phone had slipped out of the backpack and she picked it up. She found the entry in her contacts and pressed call.

"Hello, Mom? It's Ann. I'm coming home."

Loco Motive

D.M.S. Fick

If only I had feared cheese curds more and heights less, I wouldn't be running for my life through the Tracy Boxcar Days parade. Unfortunately, that's the way the cookie on a stick is crumbling today. Yes, if not for the lure of curds, my sister and I would be snug as bugs in air conditioned rugs in my cozy Tracy home, blocks away from the downtown carnival rides, and certainly not an unexpected entry in the annual parade. But our need for cheese was strong, so we journeyed to the carnival in search of grease and batter and regrets.

My sister wanted to split an order. I thought, however, that as long as we were making the effort to go to Boxcar Days, we ought to at least eat an order apiece. And, as long as we were eating cheese curds, we might as well go the distance and get snow cones, cotton candy, and mini donuts as well. Stuffed to the gills with festive confection, we waddled in our matching red T-shirts down the midway. Red T-shirts were what we always wore together in public. Our mother started the tradition so that she could find us in a crowd if we got separated from her. Now that she and Dad were both dead, we wore the T-shirts as a tribute to them, and as more than a little comfort to ourselves.

"C'mon, Sis," I said. "Let's get corn dogs too."

"Why not?" Sis replied.

No sooner were the dogs on a stick in our greedy greasy hands, than my sister pulled me with considerable might half a block down the street to a ticket booth.

"What's the big idea?" I said.

A bloodcurdling scream wrenched my attention to the sky. Before me—and above me—stood a double Ferris wheel named The Widow Maker. The ride was far too high to stand here in this normal street in this small town. It towered above the grain elevator beyond it.

"No," I said.

"Yes," she said.

I wriggled my wrist free from her grasp. She smelled fear. It was her self-appointed duty as the older sister to guide me through life. There was no way she was going to let me remain a comfortable coward.

"We're going on that Ferris wheel," Sis said.

"But we have corn dogs," I said.

"We'll eat them on the ride."

I succumbed to my sister's force because I always do—that's my self-appointed duty in life—and I usually benefit from it. I distracted myself from the menace of the ride by focusing on consuming my corn dog without redistributing its mustard to my red T-shirt or face. We stood in line behind two olive-skinned beauties. They reminded me of our aunt Helen's daughter Deb.

"Aunt Helen's going to be in the parade today," I said.

"Is she really? We have to go to the parade then, to cheer for her."

"The assisted living place she moved to has a float," I added. "It's called Oak Glade."

"I wish Mom had moved there," Sis said.

"Me too. We toured the place. It looked fun—kind of like the *Love Boat*," I said.

"Mmmhmm." My sister threw me a suggestive glance.

"Aunt Helen said the Oak Glade staff found a rare antique clock in a resident's storage bin. Margie Steen's. She left everything she had to Oak Glade when she died. I don't think they expected anything of value, but I guess this clock's worth a pretty penny. They took it to the *Antiques Cash Cow Revue* experts when they shot in Saint Paul. One of the residents has a grandson that works on the show. Turns out this clock's worth seventy-five grand. Before they took it to the *Cash Cow*, they kept it in the Happy Hour Room. When it struck five they'd all toast Margie and sing 'I'll Be Seeing You.'"

"Is it still there?" asked Sis.

"No," I said. "They put it back in the storage locker. They're waiting for some antiques dealer from the Cities to take a look at it and make an offer. They're thinking they'll use the money for a piano, maybe make some building improvements, or start an endowment. Did I mention they might get a piano?"

"Yes. That's nice, I guess. It'd be a tough call, I wager, deciding whether to keep a valuable antique or to sell it."

"They're going to buy a cuckoo clock to replace it. There's a store in New Ulm that has some pretty entertaining ones."

"Will they sing the same song when it strikes five?"

"Don't know," I said. "Maybe they'll sing 'We're in the Money.'"

I looked up at the woman whose scream had caught my attention earlier. I pondered the red car she sat in.

"I wonder if there's something wrong with that car. That woman looks scared to death."

"Only thing wrong with that car is there's a coward in it," Sis said.

I thought this was laying it on rather thick.

"I suppose you expect me to shoot Liberty Valance once we're off this ride," I proffered.

"You've got mustard on your chin," Sis said.

The red car descended to earth. The ride operator worked at the safety bar's latch. After what seemed like an hour, the bar was raised with the frightened rider still grasping it. She nearly collapsed onto the street then stumbled with her friend away from the ride and towards the patio of the municipal bar.

"The horror … the horror …" she gasped.

"Well, that appears to have been a jolly amusement for her," I said. The midway employee turned to us, smiled, and gestured to the open car. Sis pushed me ahead of her towards my doom. I put on a brave front. "What fun!" I chuckled.

The operator lowered the safety bar. He had difficulty engaging the latch. I might have interfered somehow. I kind of blacked out at some point, so I'm not sure.

"Maybe we could just hold it shut ourselves," suggested Sis. I'm not proud of this, but my right elbow, with a mind of its own, found its way to Sis's ribs.

"No, I think I should get it to stay latched," the operator said. "They were pretty specific about that in training."

Eventually, I cooperated, the latch cooperated, and the midway employee was able to secure us in the car. The Widow Maker advanced us inch by inch up into the firmament. I fussed with my corn dog so as to distract myself from our increasing elevation. By the time I was nibbling the crunchy crusty bits baked onto the wooden dowel, my sister broke my reverie.

"I think I can see your house from here," she said.

"That's impossible," I replied. "My house is five blocks away."

"Sure, and there's Sparky. Didn't you leave the dog inside the house when we left?"

"What?" I wrested my gaze from the pointed stick to where my sister indicated.

"There," she continued, "next to the car. Isn't that Sparky?"

"That's a recycling bin," I said.

"Well, it looks just like him."

"It's green."

"He's greenish, isn't he?"

"You just wanted me to stop looking at the corn dog stick and notice how far up we are."

"Well, look how splendid it all is. I didn't want you to miss it. See, there's the Asian grocery store, and there's the library, and the old Masonic Hall. Look how pretty Jacobson Park is from up here. Now put that stick away Kiddo. It's sharp. I don't want you pointing that thing in my ribs. Your elbow was bad enough."

The Widow Maker kachinked one great notch up on its cycle as another pair of riders boarded. Each time the wheel advanced, my stomach clenched and my brain fizzed. Which is worse, I wondered, the clunking stops and starts, or moving smoother but at greater speed? With three more clunks I found out.

"We're going to die!" I yelled. Now it was my sister's elbow finding purchase in my ribs.

"Quiet, Kiddo!" she exclaimed. "You'll frighten the children."

That worked. I fell silent.

We zipped around the axis, then were launched into the atmosphere like a clown's juggling clubs. The second wheel plummeted to earth to disgorge its passengers and load up new fools. Did I mention that this was a double Ferris wheel? Did I mention that all double Ferris wheels are evil? I palpated my stomach to see if it was indeed still there or if it was now twenty feet behind me like it felt it was.

"You're a mean sister," I pouted. I fought to hold in my tears.

"Stop being such a baby," Sis chided. "Look! There's Oak Glade. I wonder which window is Aunt Helen's."

My eyes followed where she pointed. Looking off into the distance was better than looking straight down. I could fool myself into thinking I was inside a sturdy building or atop a very solid mountain, instead of suspended in air pondering my mortality.

"I think she mentioned her apartment was in the front," I said. "Second floor maybe. Oh, someone's coming out the front door. It's not Helen, though. It's two people. Huh, they're in red T-shirts like us. Small world. They're carrying something, putting it in a red convertible. I don't know where they think they're going. They're blocked in all directions by the parade route, and it starts in fifteen minutes." The car lurched, interrupting my fascinating commentary. I pitched forward against the safety bar. I screamed—a scream that outscreamed the curdler's scream—a scream that was heard for miles, even by Sparky the Recycling Bin—a scream heard by the person who'd just exited the Oak Glade Living Center. He looked right up at us. Sis was still pointing and I was still screaming.

"Stop screaming, Kiddo," she said. "They'll kick us off the ride." Our motivations were probably a little mismatched here. I continued screaming. The Oak Glade visitor stopped looking at us and got in the red convertible. A gap opened up momentarily in the parade. The red convertible merged into it and moved away from Oak Glade along with the other parade units.

The ride operator brought our wheel back to loading position and advanced to our car.

"See! They're kicking us off," Sis said.

I stopped screaming. A beatific calm spread throughout by body. I think I glowed.

"I don't know why you're so scared," Sis continued. "They keep these rides in perfectly safe operating condition. It's their business, you know, not their hobby. There are regulations." This made so much sense to me now that my feet were again on the pavement. "Let's get out of here," Sis said. "We need to find a spot to watch the parade."

I was still unsettled enough by my near-death experience that Sis had to guide me through the crowds. We ended up in front of St. Mary's School. It was a popular spot for parade-goers. Inside the school was a flea market. Outside, a food stand sold burgers, brats, and footlongs beneath a shady marquee. Sis parked me under a benevolent elm tree.

"Stay here, Kiddo. I'll go get us some burgers."

"Oh good," I replied. "I am feeling a bit peckish." Did I mention it had been a good ten minutes since I'd last eaten?

The parade started while Sis was at the tent. The Tracy Area High

School Panthers marched toward me playing the "Minnesota Rouser." I applauded along with the proud parents and other band enthusiasts. I noticed colorful splotches of squashed candy on the road and wondered about the soles of the musicians' shoes. My heart skipped a beat when I looked up again because following the band was a red convertible. The driver waved. The passenger threw candy. Whew! It was only the mayor, but it reminded me I had a civic duty to perform.

"I wonder if anything shady was going on at Oak Glade. Perhaps I should call the police just in case. It would hurt nothing for an officer to check it out," I said to myself.

I pulled my cell phone from a pocket. The corn dog stick came out with it. I was distracted by a parade mascot in a squirrel costume carrying a giant papier-mâché acorn. Next in line was a clown juggling clubs. Behind the clown was another red convertible. A sign on the door said, RED'S ANTIQUES & COLLECTIBLES. The driver wore a red T-shirt. He glared at me, then looked beyond me and gave a quick nod.

"Put the phone away, Missy," a voice hissed into my ear. "We're going for a ride."

The red convertible stopped in front of me. The man behind me pressed what might have been a gun into my back and nudged me towards the car.

My heart did a Skip To My Lou as my thoughts travelled back to my childhood. Sis and I were standing on the back of our dad's tractor while the spray tank behind it was being filled with a garden hose. Dad was inside the house. A car of suspicious men pulled up to the tractor.

"Come with us," the driver said in my memory. "We know where the leftover Easter-egg-hunt candy is."

I started to move off the tractor. I liked candy. My sister grabbed my arm.

"Never get into the car, Kiddo," she'd said. Her vice-like grip had told me I was staying by her side on the tractor.

I snapped back to the present.

"Never get in the car," I murmured. I swung around and jabbed my corndog stick into the potential abductor's abdomen. He doubled over. I swung around again, dove into the parade and barreled against the current. I ran past the juggling clown, past the squirrel with the giant nut. In the distance I could see the Oak Glade float. I felt if I could just reach Aunt Helen I'd be safe. Did I dare look behind me? The title music from

Chariots of Fire danced in my head. I kept my gaze forward. I saw Aunt Helen's concerned face drawing nearer. Beside her stood a sturdy woman in a nurse's uniform.

"Up here!" called the Oak Glade nurse. We clasped hands and she pulled me up onto the float. Aunt Helen gave me a benevolent smile for just a second before drawing up a large tote bag of candy. With the strength and skill of David, she swung her weapon and clocked the staggering goon squarely on the temple. He spun round and was bounced into the oncoming marching band. The banner carriers promptly ran their sign round him, securing him into a tightly wound cocoon. The tuba player finished the job by capping him with his horn.

But where was the driver in the red convertible? I looked up the parade route in time to see my sister grab the giant papier-mâché acorn from the squirrel. She jumped into the passenger seat of the convertible and beaned the driver hard on the noggin causing him to collapse forward onto the steering wheel. A shower of saltwater taffy burst forth like fireworks about his ears. My sister placed a foot on the brake and shifted the transmission to park. The crowd cheered and rushed the car to assist her. Sis reached into the back seat. Lo and behold, she stood up with the antique clock and raised it high above her head like a trophy, as befit the hero she was and always will be. Did I mention how glad I am that she's my sister?

No Time Like the Present

E.B. Boatner

"Come be our guest at Twin Cities Pride," Wade's note invited. "We want you to share this special time with us." How could I refuse? My uncle Wade was not only my godfather, but he and his partner, Eli, took me in after Father found out I was gay.

It was pushing 87 degrees as I chained my bike and walked towards the corner of Ninth and Hennepin. We'd arranged to meet at ten, upstairs in Crave, and Wade had assured me we'd view the Parade *indoors*, with AC and Mojitos. I was almost to Hennepin when the very air shimmered and a couple appeared in front of me in the milling crowd. They could have stepped straight out of an Evelyn Waugh novel and were eccentric even by Pride sartorial standards. The man was about my height, a few inches over six feet, and the woman nearly his match.

I may dress like an Ivy League hobo, but I'd grown up in an unhealthily wealthy, socially dysfunctional family, so the outfits struck me as odd only that no one in Minneapolis, dressed in top hats and frock coats, would stroll like mad dogs out in the noonday sun. Impeccably tailored, the gent's swallowtails parted as he walked, revealing striped morning sponge-bag trousers, and his gleaming patent leather pumps beneath their pearl-grey spats, struck sparks of reflected sunlight.

His companion wore a huge, wide-brimmed, cream straw hat raked over her left ear, adorned simply with an emerald green band and a single, swooping back feather. Diaphanous sleeves of a mysterious, nearly non-fabric billowed from her shoulders then clasped at her wrists. Sunlight penetrated the loose weave to outline a supple body sheathed in an Art Deco ecru lace frock that flowed down over her boyish hips. I'd spent much of my boyhood swanking about on the sly in Mother's party frocks. I *know* how sheer dresses flow over boyish hips.

Hindered momentarily by a ruffled sash, the dress paused before cascading to just below the woman's knees. The fabric's movement accentuated her long legs and trim ankles. She strode serenely, her slender feet shod in off-white satin T-strap pumps.

Mesmerized, I pulled out my camera and snapped at their retreating backs. I longed to push in front to capture their faces, but held back out of an uncharacteristic respect for their privacy. I did my best, though as usual I couldn't really see the digital screen in the sun's glare.

At the corner of Hennepin, I lost sight of them as the couple melted into the swarms of people hurrying now to clear the street and claim good vantage points for the parade. As I paused at the corner, I caught a glimpse of the topper and feather disappearing into Solera.

❂

"Are we having fun yet?" I called out to Wade and Eli, ensconced at a window table.

"*We* are," replied Wade, looking up from his half-empty Mojito—half-*full*, my inexorably cheerful relative would see it. "*You're* not expected to go that far. Just be agreeable."

Wade and Eli rose from their chairs, and I went around and we exchanged hugs. At 70 and 72, my uncles are as vital as they had been when I'd lived with them twenty-something years ago. They still biked and swam and made a point of walking several miles a day whatever the weather.

"It's hot," I grumbled.

"It's June," Eli pointed out, "and it's cool in here. Sit down."

Wade filled a third glass from their lime-laden pitcher, pushed it over to me, and swept his arm in a broad arc. "It's Twin Cities Pride 2013! History's in the making! Gay marriage is alive in the land, and DOMA is *dead.*"

"And you want to be committed in matrimony?" I stopped short, remembering that Wade and Eli had been together some thirty years, longer than had my own long-divorced parents.

"As a matter of fact, we do, Edmund. Drink up. We've got a wait yet. Eli insisted on a good view, and we wanted you to see this." Wade pulled a paper out of an envelope and waved it at me.

"Your wedding license! That's wonderful, you two! When's the happy day?"

"August first," they replied in unison. "The very first day we can," finished Wade, beaming at me, and then at Eli, with such a look of love that it tugged at my heartstrings.

"And look here!" I exclaimed in my eagerness, turning the spotlight back on *me*. "Wait'll you see these two—I was following them just now—" I turned the camera on and turned the screen to them.

"What? Who?" Wade and Eli cast glances at one another, then at me.

"The two in the Edwardian outfits … " I looked; they weren't there. A sea of backs, a small open space, lots of party costumes, but no top hat and feather.

"I don't understand. I've messed up outdoor shots when I can't see the screen, but I always catch *something*."

"Don't worry about it, son. Maybe you'll run into them again later," Wade soothed. "Just remember to save that date. You're the designated best man, and even my august brother and your lady mother have deigned," Eli elbowed him in the ribs, and Wade amended, "have graciously accepted our invitation. No snide remarks, Edmund."

Far from snide remarks, I was moved, unable to say anything at all. I picked up the camera bag and went over to the window, my back turned, blinking a time or two.

But I couldn't get that couple out of my mind. I looked across at Solera's rooftop, and there they were, in the near corner.

"Ed!" Eli called, sounding as peevish as his nature would allow. "Did you hear what I just said?"

My attention stayed riveted on the rooftop. I pulled out my 300mm lens, swapped it for the 50mm on the Canon, and zoomed in. I could see them clearly now, but that only raised more questions. The two were obviously older up close than I'd estimated earlier. Eerily old, but not *elderly*, they had an ageless, *timeless* quality that spoke of somewhere far beyond the classic garments they wore so effortlessly.

Then the woman turned towards me, her green-eyed gaze filling the lens that linked us. I lowered the camera. Too late: she had bid me come.

What excuse I gave to my uncles I couldn't tell you. I shook off Eli's hand as I rushed past and hastened downstairs into the crowd, weaving across the avenue to Solera. It was cooler inside, though crammed to the gills with late breakfasters, brunchers, and consumers of cold and colorful drinks. A familiar place, I went there often for post-theatre beers and post-mortems of the evening's show. I knew where the elevators led to the roof, but pushed instead to the stairway and took them two at a time. I hesitated at the door. What if I'd misread her look? I'm not butch by a long shot, nor am I usually fearful, but I was afraid. I waited for a sign. Nada. I took a deep breath and pushed out onto the patio under the blazing sun, caught up in the shouts and laughter and the clink of cutlery and glasses.

They were on the far side of a stand of potted shrubs and flowers, standing shoulder to shoulder at a tall bar table. Neither turned, but I was certain that she sensed my presence. As I drew near, the surrounding air became a cool oasis infused with a pungent odor. *Cypress*, a poignant and particular memory of a summer in Greece with Wade and Eli when I was eighteen. I closed my eyes and opened them to find I was being drawn into hers.

"Thank you for coming," she murmured calmly, as though welcoming me into her home. She tipped that magnificent hat a degree and a waiter appeared, placed a tall, frosted glass in front of me, and melted into the crowd. I took a long pull on what I'd declare was the best mint julep ever constructed north of Churchill Downs.

I had barely felt the glass hit the table when the noise and laughter faded, and I was plunging down, down, into darkness. I shivered in what felt like an autumn chill. I was standing upright in front of the building I'd entered a few minutes earlier. Right *here*—on the corner of Hennepin and Ninth, dark and deserted at whatever late hour it was. No sign of late diners, theatergoers, or passersby.

Someone shrieked in pain.

I hastened around the corner, beyond the theater's exit doors, and came upon a gang of toughs with two youths in formal attire. Two restrained one victim, forcing him to watch while three more assaulted the other, punching his face and belly. Hideous pains tore through my own head and gut with each blow. I screamed, but made no sound; I tried to move forward to help, but could not move.

The thugs took no notice of my presence, and when their victim slumped to the ground, attempting to shield his face with his arms, they continued with their feet, their boots landing sickening blows on his skull and ribs.

I was pinioned as securely as those young men, suffering their phantom, yet palpable agony.

When the beaten boy ceased to move and lay twisted against the brick wall, his dress hat crushed in the dirt, the three turned their attentions on the other terrified youth, pushing their two cohorts aside and methodically beating the lad while cursing and calling "pervert," "sodomite," and other vile epithets, taking care not to call too loudly and draw attention. Their two companions had drawn back against the wall, looked on with excitement and fear until both boys lay broken and still, their bodies reduced to dark smudges against the pavement.

I was finally able to move. My own pain was gone. I started forward, intent on helping, but the street was empty. I shouted for help, but my words were snatched away in a dark wind, and I was once more standing at the table, blinking in the heat and hullabaloo, drenched in a cold sweat. My hand closed on the beaded julep glass and lifted it to my lips. I took a fortifying draught, letting the smoky bourbon do its work.

The woman, eyes bright under the hat brim's shadow, waited until I had pulled myself into some semblance of order and stated, "You saw." It was not a question.

"Was that …" I looked to her companion who had not yet spoken a word. He turned his face towards mine, eyes as impenetrable as a forest pool. He nodded but kept silent.

"My brother Anthony. My twin," she amended, and I felt foolish not to have realized their consanguinity. Their height, the fine bone structure, the green, green eyes. "Andrea." She bowed imperceptibly, introducing herself to me, despite my silence.

"What just happened?" I managed to ask after another deep swallow that drained the glass. Again, the waiter swooped in and in one fluid motion removed my empty and set a second icy drink in its place.

"My brother and his dear friend, Jeffrey," Andrea continued, "were here one night, a long time ago. They'd dressed to the nines, had dinner together and gone to the new Hennepin Theatre that had opened a few days earlier." She inclined her head slightly and I realized she meant the Orpheum, next door.

"It was a special evening also because the Marx Brothers were performing. Tony loved them, adored all vaudeville and comedy—my brother had a marvelous sense of humor. Father intended for him to go to Harvard as he and *his* father had done. Tony didn't care about the courses, but he was keen to write for the *Lampoon*.

"I was to go with them that night, but Mother was recovering from influenza. Father was out of town so I assured her I'd keep her company.

We both urged the boys to go on, there were dinner reservations and the tickets were already bought."

"And it was Jeffrey's eighteenth birthday." Anthony's voice made me jump and Andrea reached for his hand. We waited, but he said no more.

"If only I had been there." Andrea spoke barely above a whisper. Her voice rose and hardened. "There were five against two. Tony and Jeff never had a chance. I *know*." She forestalled my question. "I saw it all through Tony's eyes."

"I heard what those thugs called them," I began.

"Perverts. Sodomites. I know those words," she added at my shocked expression. "They were those things in the eyes of others. Not mine. I loved seeing Tony happy, though I worried about their future together— I knew they were more than just friends."

She looked past my shoulder into some place I could not follow, then turned back, eyes blazing.

"I was *there*. I woke late at night and saw it all, heard it all. Then it was over and too late to help. Of course, no one believed me when I spoke out later. I was seventeen, a *girl*, hysterical about her brother. My words were not used as evidence and they never caught the men. Not even my parents knew that Anthony and I could ... *transmit*, I suppose you'd say. That evening was the strongest, the most complete sharing we'd ever experienced. It was horrible."

This time Anthony put his hand over hers. "Tell him."

"Our parents were devastated more by learning that Anthony was what Father called an "invert" than by his terrible injuries and suffering. And because it put paid to his dream of a son carrying on the Harvard tradition. You see, only the year before, President Lowell had instigated a terrible purge of homosexuals in the college; at least two young men committed suicide, careers were ruined. There was no way for Anthony to attend once the incident became known.

"My father saw to it that the assault was reported as an 'attempted robbery,' but some of his old classmates learned the true story. Father withdrew Anthony's application. Jeffrey's family moved away with him as soon as he could travel. Anthony never found a trace of Jeffrey; no letters ever came. They never set eyes on one another again.

"I could do nothing until I passed over, which was not long after. Ironically, Mother lived into her eighties, Anthony recovered physically, but I, the athletic one, succumbed to the flu the following fall."

"But why did you call me? What can I do?" I was both distraught and puzzled. "All this is monstrous, but it happened so long ago."

"Time has no meaning here. I learn things in tiny increments, but I have to work through the living, in their time. You're alive; you can see. You can help me end this thread of suffering."

"But why me? What have I got to do with all this?" I took a quick sip, noticing that my companions did not touch their own drinks.

"I wanted revenge and found it easier to obtain dead than alive. It was not difficult to arrange that the three that did the beating found dangerous careers; it was 1921 and bootlegging was rife in Minnesota. They all died young and violently. One of the two observers deeply regretted his participation—he was barely sixteen, out for a thrill. When his only son died at Monte Casino I felt no need to exact further suffering.

"The fifth prospered, lived long and tried to repress the episode, telling himself it was 'just boys roughhousing and an unfortunate accident'. But he never spoke of the incident to his wife or sons, and, as often as it was in my power, I filled his dreams with the crunch of boots on bones, the cries of the victims.

"His son was a tough, hard-nosed business man, and *his* issue—and now I'm getting closer to the answer to your question—consisted of two sons, one of whom, named Wade, turned out to be a boy just like Anthony and Jeffrey. And then I found out something about my own father."

She must have seen my look of blank incomprehension, for she explained, "Time doesn't exist here, and what we learn is not linear. Anthony predeceased our parents; he never fully lived again without Jeffrey. I was at his bedside while he lay dying. My spirit was with my brother. It was not until another time that I remembered that Father had taken a box from the back of an old cupboard and burned the contents in the incinerator behind the garage. I went back. I saw. That box was filled with scores of letters from Jeffrey."

Anthony's head snapped up, his eyes bright with the very look I'd seen in Wade's when he'd smiled at Eli not an hour earlier.

"Jeffrey loves me! Why did you never—"

"In this world, dear, you'd say I just found out. And I feared to raise your hopes. She looked up and nodded across the way where I could make out the figures of Wade and Eli, and a third figure, close to the window, chatting.

"He was supposed to meet us *here*," Andrea laughed. "But Jeffrey's sense of time and space weren't the best even in a world where those existed."

Anthony was already heading for the door.

❁

"Where've you been?" Wade grabbed my elbow. "We've met the most delightful young man…and so have you, I see." He winked at Anthony, who nodded and brushed past to embrace Jeffrey.

"Come along," said Andrea, "Edmund will explain later, the parade's—" Her words were swallowed by a phalanx of Dykes on Bikes roaring by.

The Wheelman

Jeanne Mulcare

It was a beautiful June Saturday, and, as expected, Deputy Gilbert Peltier had missed his tee time. His golf bag, shoved in the back seat, rattled when he brought his car to a stop behind his partner Janke's dented, unmarked squad. Across the street sat the crime lab vehicle; beyond it, two patrol cars hemmed in a catering van.

The door to the garage was open and Gilbert eyeballed the interior as he walked past. A cobalt blue BMW convertible, top down, was parked directly in the center of the two-car garage. Signs attached to the sides of the car indicated it had been used by Miss Columbia Heights 1998, sponsor of the Columbia Heights Jamboree coronation and pageant. He snapped a photo with his cell phone, then stepped back from the garage to take in the expansive Greek Revival house attached to it. Miss Columbia Heights 1998 had done okay for herself.

He proceeded down a set of flagstone steps to the back, where white tea lights strung from a large maple tree shimmered against the surface of a small pool nearby. Several tables were set with white linen, and on the center table rested an old gramophone. An evening of mint juleps and Oysters Rockefeller was in somebody's future.

Caterers prepared food in the nearby pool house. If they knew Deputy Peltier was there, they gave no indication. He continued down the steps to the shoreline of a small bay. Deputy Ray Janke, his partner, stood waiting for him near a body floating face down. The dead man's jeans looked stained and the cuffs were ragged.

Janke glanced around at the nouveau riche homes with finely manicured lawns. "This guy's a little out of place don't you think?"

"Day not going good for you, Ray?" Janke's face, usually deadpan under such circumstances, looked downright pissed.

"I'm having flashbacks from my own pretentious upbringing, and the homeowner, Michael Burton, was trying to lay the ground rules.

We've been told to hurry the investigation along and move out before the party."

"He said that?" Gilbert asked.

"Not him directly. He called the head of the homeowners association and that guy called the dispatcher, who called me."

Gilbert brought his sunglasses down to look directly into Janke's eyes. "So who found the body?"

"Burton. He called it in, and when Deputy Flood arrived, he pointed to one of the caterers and told him to—," Janke looked at his notebook, "escort the police down to the shore of the lake."

"He was probably upset," Gilbert said.

"Of course he's upset. He's got a body stinking up his property, and now we've got a possible murder in a fiefdom where crime doesn't exist."

Gilbert looked around. "Where's Burton now?"

"At the house. I've made him Flood's problem."

Both men looked down at the body. It was floating naked from the waist up. From just beneath the water, a murky tattoo of a Texas longhorn glared at them. The senior member of the forensic team, William Tan, grabbed the jeans and started moving the body.

Gilbert stopped him. "Let me get some pictures for my file."

"Oh, I assure you deputy, there isn't a square inch of real estate on this body's backside that we haven't photographed. He'd be in the wagon but for your friend, who said we should hang around until you got here."

Tan appeared calm enough but Gilbert knew better. Keeping him waiting was not a good idea. Janke once said that crossing Tan was like sticking a hand in a sewer drain for car keys and hoping that you didn't end up petting a ten-pound rat.

Gilbert shut off his phone and put it back in his pocket. "I'm here now. We can start," he said.

"There's lividity." Tam kneeled down in the water next to Gilbert and pointed to bruising across the victim's back. The blood had pooled mostly on the right side. He picked up a hand, brought it up to the surface to examine it, then let go gently.

He added. "The body's been here only a short time. Any longer with this heat, we'd be spooning him out with a giant ladle."

Janke said what they both were thinking. "He was hauled in."

Tan nodded. "With the lividity, that would be my guess. His face is down now, but most of the discoloration is on the backside. So that means the body was moved after he died."

Tan moved the body closer to the shoreline and carefully turned it over, freeing two small dead fish trapped beneath it.

"Bullheads," Janke said. "I should tell the caterers."

Gilbert squinted into the watery shadows. Under the muck of weeds rose the faint lines of another tattoo.

The photographer came up from behind and Gilbert heard a camera fire in rapid succession. He rolled up his pant legs and squatted down, forgoing concern for his beat-up shoes.

The brim of Gilbert's backward-facing cap touched his shoulders and lifted up. He pushed it down to keep it from falling into the water, then tilted his head to get a better view. A hole the size of navy bean had opened up a cavity in the left chest area.

Janke squatted beside Gilbert, and Tan pointed to the hole in the chest. "Our vic's been shot." He pushed Gilbert aside and looked up at the photographer. "Get a close up."

Gilbert traced the lines again with his finger without touching the body. "I think it's a Ferris wheel."

"Leave it to Gil to examine the artwork," Tan said. He carefully splashed water against the spot to remove debris and then leaned aside for the tech to take more shots. An old time Ferris wheel materialized with a bullet hole in the center.

Gilbert turned his head and looked up at his partner. Janke's attention was elsewhere. "Gawkers."

A boat came into the bay but stayed on the far side. Gilbert had had enough of the stench. He stood up and wiped at his face, took his hat off, brushed his straight black hair back with the crook of his arm, then put the cap back on with the brim facing forward this time. The badge on his belt shone. He grabbed his phone and snapped a photo. The boat sped away. Tan had been watching it too. Its wake rolled toward them, and its impact rocked the body back and forth against Tan's legs.

Gilbert turned to see a man coming towards them. Somehow Burton had escaped Deputy Flood. He was wearing a crisp white shirt and linen slacks.

"Sir, I'm going to have to ask you to go back to the house," Gilbert said.

"We have a party planned for this afternoon," Burton said.

Gilbert looked up and stared at the man. "You were instructed to stay with the deputy."

"I own this property."

"You're compromising an investigation."

When Deputy Flood reappeared, Burton grudgingly walked away with him. Gilbert went back to work.

Tan pulled a wallet from the victim's pocket. He handed it to Gilbert. Gilbert fished through it and found a Minnesota Class A commercial driver's license. The man in the photo had a nice smile and friendly green eyes.

"Anthony Dover. Date of birth is May sixteen." Gilbert looked down at the tattoo of the bull again. "His birth sign, Taurus the bull."

"The wagon's here." Janke was back.

While Janke called in the name for warrants, Gilbert found a business card. Midway Carnival Corporation. "Looks like somebody lost their wheelman," he said.

Janke and Gilbert both noticed a woman step onto the porch. She was tall and slender, and from a distance quite beautiful.

"Is that the wife?" Gilbert asked.

"Mrs. Oksana Burton, I presume."

"Oksana. Sounds foreign," Gilbert said.

"I think it's Eastern European," Janke said.

Janke handed Dover's license over to a forensic guy who was bagging the evidence. "He's clean. Good driving record. No state priors."

Gilbert removed his evidence gloves. "You need to put a call through to Columbia Heights. There's a car in the garage with banners from their parade."

"What?"

"The garage was open when I walked by. I think that woman," Gilbert nodded in Oksana Burton's direction, "was Miss Columbia Heights 1998. I'm willing to bet that she was at their Jamboree last night. With every jamboree—"

"Comes a carnival. And with every carnival there's a Ferris wheel," Janke said.

Gilbert threw his evidence gloves in a bag and walked up the hill to where Burton was standing. Everything about the man was paid for except for one imperfection—a small scar above the right eyebrow.

"I'm Deputy Peltier, Mr. Burton. There's a car in your garage that's been decorated for the Columbia Heights parade."

"I know what's in my garage. Your associate was given instructions to leave within an hour and that hour was an hour ago."

"Who was in the parade?"

"Your job is to remove that body." He pointed in the direction of the victim without looking.

"Certainly you realize this is bigger than your party."

"How?"

Gilbert shook his head and pulled out his notebook. "Who found the body?"

"You already know that or you wouldn't even be here," Burton said.

He stared into the man's eyes. "I'm going to ask the question again. Who found the body?"

Gilbert watched unease wash over Burton, changing him from a Grand Poobah to what seemed like a quivering schoolboy being scolded for stealing from a lunchbox.

"Again, this is a waste of time, but I'll repeat what I said earlier. I went out for a run this morning and saw something along the shoreline. It looked like a body so I called the police."

Gilbert had been looking over Burton's shoulder as Janke interviewed the caterers. They were pointing at the ground in the center of the property and soon Janke was moving the techs up to the area. Burton turned around to see what the commotion was about.

Gilbert pointed to the lake where the body was being placed in a body bag. "You still want to stick to the story that you found it there?"

Burton's eyes shifted in the direction of the caterers and then back to the water. Gilbert let him watch the men move the bag around the body and zip it up.

"Where was the body, Mr. Burton? We both know it got moved."

Burton looked away from the lake and kept his eyes down as he spoke. He gestured to where Janke and techs were working. "About there."

"So, not at the property line, but directly in front of your house?" Gilbert asked.

"We are having a party."

Gilbert watched as the forensic team expanded the search. The yellow tape would now stretch across the entire shoreline.

"How did you move the body?"

Shame began to seep into Burton's face. "The pole for cleaning the pool."

Gilbert was happy to see a semblance of conscience but didn't detect any empathy for the victim. "We're taking it into evidence."

"I shouldn't have, but he was dead."

"You compromised an investigation. Did you know the victim?"

Burton's eyes flashed. "Him? No. Of course I didn't know him. Would I leave him here if I did?"

Gilbert and Burton stared up the hill. Mrs. Burton was walking towards the pool.

"That's my wife and she's not involved in this business. She slept in. She'd been working the coronation for Jamboree Days in Columbia Heights and, yes, she was in the parade last night. She's exhausted. Leave her alone."

"Why Columbia Heights? You don't live there."

Burton seemed to soften. "Before I met Oksana, when she was nineteen, she was crowned Miss Columbia Heights."

"And?"

"She told me it saved her life. I couldn't imagine something so frivolous saving a person's life, but it did. A former queen took Oksana under her wing, a Jamboree sponsor found her a place to live, and they both encouraged her to go to college. My wife feels deeply indebted. She does anything she can to help the Jamboree. The party today is for the volunteers. Afterwards, she'll go back to Murzyn Hall for this year's coronation."

"Was she at the carnival?"

"She's a chaperone. The candidates were there, so yes she was."

"Did you hear about any problems last night?"

He shrugged nonchalantly. "She mentioned something, but whatever it was ended quickly. Just a shove, a few words. Security came and got the man to move along. It's not so unusual."

"Was it the guy you found floating in the water?"

"I wasn't at the festivities last night, so I can't say."

Gilbert asked Burton about his neighbors. Burton told him that most families on the bay chose this time of year to go on vacation.

"Do you have an alarm system?"

"We all do."

Gilbert pointed toward a small wooded area full of bushes and river willows on the east side of his property. Tan and the techs had started going through it. "Is that an easement?"

Burton had been watching the progress. "Yes."

"No alarms in that area, right?"

Burton didn't answer for a moment. "No. It's association property."

Oksana walked towards them. She stopped and gave Burton a look. Both husband and wife knew a lot more than they were letting on.

Tan whistled and Gilbert saw him pull back the bushes. Janke joined them. The techs pulled out something large and put it in a bag.

"What is that?" Burton asked.

"I might ask you the same thing," Gilbert said.

"We did nothing."

Gilbert climbed down towards the easement.

"They found a blanket," Janke said. "It's damp with last night's rain, but it's covered in blood and hair. They also found a receipt for a set of tires and an inhaler with the victim's name on it."

"Anything else?" Gilbert asked.

"Not much. The rains last night wiped out any evidence of shoe tracks." He stopped and looked at his phone. "I've got Heights PD calling."

Gilbert waited for Janke to finish the call.

"That was Officer Renke over at Heights police station. Anthony Dover is missing. He worked as a mechanic for Midway Carnival which contracts every year with the Jamboree."

"Any known connection to the Burtons?"

"Renke told me that last night Dover got involved in a scuffle involving Mrs. Burton and her father, who in Renke's opinion is a nut case. Dover called security, a couple of off duties, and they ushered the old man out of the place.

"It seems that daddy was one Milan Zebin, a former Soviet Union gangster they dumped on us twenty-five years ago. He came here with his wife and ten-year-old daughter, Oksana. Some local churches had a deal going with our government to sponsor Russian families who were suffering from religious persecution. And the Soviets were only too happy to get rid of one of their more notorious thugs. This guy's always been trouble.

"Zebin's neighbors think he killed their dogs, and they're pretty sure he burned down a shed that he thought crossed over his property line."

"Does Oksana have a relationship with him?"

"Absolutely not. She's got a restraining order against Zebin. Renke says back in Russia, Oksana saw him kill a man with his bare hands."

Tan had been listening in. "Can she ID the blanket?"

Mr. and Mrs. Burton approached the group and they all fell silent. Oksana Burton's eyes grew large when she saw the bag. It was slightly open. She shook her head and her hand flew to her chest. Burton put his arm around wife's shoulders.

"I know what this is about. He follows me like a shadow. My mother and I tried to leave him behind but the Soviet government said either he went or none of us did. So of course we all came," Oksana Burton said.

Janke picked up the bag. "Mrs. Burton, we want you to look at a blanket. Tell us if you recognize it."

Her eyes moved down his arm to the bag. He opened it and she peered in.

"Ah," she said as if all the pieces suddenly fell into place. "Men know nothing. It's a quilt. My mother made it for me when I was a child. I asked for it when she died." She closed her eyes. "You see, he's finally returned it."

Janke's voice was soft. "Oksana, who returned it?"

"Milan Zebin, my father."

A Killer in the Cornfield

Cathlene N. Buchholz

Although my little brother had found the body behind the restaurant's dumpster, I was the one who was traumatized. "Over here," Jack's voice had squeaked with excitement. I hurried across the parking lot in a hoodie zipped up to my throat, my stiff fingers poking out of the sleeves. It was late afternoon in our little southern Minnesota town, and October had been threatening snow.

I glanced down at the large figure sprawled next to Jack's feet. He wasn't quite dead. But then again, he had never been quite alive. Even so, someone had plunged a knife into his chest and blobbed on red paint for effect. Most of the body's stuffing had been ripped out and scattered across the asphalt.

With tear-filled eyes, I removed the weapon and laid it on the ground away from Jack's feet. I had hoped to win this year's scarecrow contest and use the prize money to buy an iPod. Plus Dad was counting on me to win. Every fall, he boasted of the first place scarecrow he had built. Even Jack had been a winner one year with Dad's help.

"It's up to you," Dad had said. "If you put in the effort, we can make this a family tradition."

I pulled my thoughts back to the parking lot and looked down at what my effort had gotten me.

"It'll be okay, Samantha." Jack's tongue lisped around the "s" in my name. I couldn't help but smile.

Jack was right. We could rebuild him; we had the technology. He and I stuffed the straw back into the man's chest and straightened the wires in his bionic limbs. Jack pushed and I pulled as we dragged the six-foot scarecrow back to the cornfield of straw men behind the restaurant. We propped him into place and wired him to his fence post. I made an adjustment to his metal kneecaps, and then stood back.

"I'll get the knife." Jack turned to run.

"No." I grabbed the sleeve of his purple jacket before he and the fierce Viking embroidered on his back got too far. "Don't touch it. We'll tell Mrs. Crumble."

Mr. and Mrs. Crumble owned the Esther Crumble's Restaurant. But it was mostly Mrs. Crumble who ran it. Her husband puttered around in the apple orchard and pumpkin patch. "Howdy do?" he'd greet us. He also organized the Esther Crumble's Annual Scarecrow Festival, pounding in fence posts for a hundred exhibits.

Mrs. Crumble stood next to the bakery display, setting out pies. "Oh, heavens," she said when we told her about the knife. Jack dropped to the floor and flailed his arms and legs, showing her how the scarecrow had looked.

"And someone had … had *killed* him," he said.

"Is that so?" She stuck out her hand and helped Jack to his feet. "Well, I'm glad you rescued him. It wouldn't be a fair contest with one scarecrow missing in action." She patted our shoulders. "I'll take care of that nasty knife. And don't you kids worry. The volunteers don't judge until Friday. You have plenty of time to fix up your little man." She winked at me over Jack's head.

❀

Although the scarecrow display closed each day at six, my friend, Becca, met me in the cornfield after supper to witness the damage. She aimed her flashlight at the scarecrow's ripped shirt and then dabbed at the dried paint with her fingertip. "What about Mr. Austin's mortal wound?" She's been referring to my entry as Mr. Austin ever since I'd come up with the notion of having a bionic scarecrow.

"I'll get some more wires and stick them out of his chest. It'll look even better than before." I smiled at Becca, but she only rolled her eyes.

Dad had supplied most of the material, not only clothes and sneakers but also metal scraps from his welding shop. "He looks like a cross between the Terminator and Steve Austin," he'd said of my finished product. "You did a good job. He's better, stronger, faster." *The Six Million Dollar Man* had been a favorite show when he was a kid. Dad mimicked running in slow motion and then stopped to throw pretend punches at me.

"Earth to Sam," Becca's voice interrupted my thoughts. She stood in the moonlight with her arms folded across her flat chest, her red hair blowing wildly about her face. "Any clues who the killer is?"

"Not really." My eyes stung from the wind and I shivered. "I'm just glad Jack found him and we were able to fix him up."

"Yeah, lucky you." She spun around and followed the path that zig-zagged through the field. I kept close behind. Becca's light flashed left and right, bouncing off outstretched arms, toothless grins, and unblinking eyes. "You know," she said, aiming the beam on the last entry, "it could've been the boys."

The boys she referred to were Drew and Josh. Drew had a crush on me and everyone knew it. What they didn't know was that I liked him back. Not even Becca knew that.

As we stared at the last entry—Drew and Josh's entry—Becca snorted. "What a bunch of losers." She poked at the masked scarecrow dressed in red-splattered scrubs. A toy stethoscope dangled around his neck. Bent over a Frankenstein-looking scarecrow that lay supine across two sawhorses, he gripped a plastic saw in his gloved hands.

"Actually, it's kind of cool," I said. The boys were into the old black and white horror films—anything to do with the early monsters of Hollywood. Last Halloween, they'd chased us in their werewolf costumes, howling like idiots. I had half-hoped Drew would catch me.

Becca nudged the scarecrow's blue shoe cover with her toe. "Mine was much better." She was referring to her entry from last year—Bella and Edward scarecrows from *Twilight* that hadn't even placed. I'd had to console her for weeks.

"I'm glad I didn't enter this dumb contest again." She handed me the flashlight and blew her nose. As she turned to walk back, I flashed the light at the plastic saw.

❀

"We didn't do anything," Drew said, his face red. Drew was the biggest kid in sixth grade, not only tall big, but also plump big. We stood on his doorstep as he and Becca argued through the screen door.

"Yeah, right." Becca planted her hand on her bony hip. "And I suppose Mr. Austin just decided to walk behind the dumpster, whip out a knife, and do himself in?"

Josh stood behind Drew, laughing hysterically, until Drew elbowed him in his skinny gut. "Honest, Sam. We didn't touch your scarecrow."

I half-believed him despite Josh's wide smile.

As Jack and I waited at the bus stop the next morning, we looked up the hill for Becca. The bus appeared from the opposite direction and rumbled toward us.

"There she is!" Jack pointed at the running figure. Becca arrived out of breath just as the bus stopped and squeaked open its door.

"Mr. Austin's gone!" she panted, grabbing my arm.

Jack stared at her, his mouth open.

"All aboard," the driver said.

"Go on, Jack." I prodded him up the steps. Becca and I followed, heading to the back row. "What happened?" I asked.

Jack popped his head over his seat like a gopher.

"Dad was having coffee at the restaurant and Mr. Crumble came in. He said that a mischief maker had been in the cornfield." Becca slumped back and sighed dramatically. "I ran down there to take a look."

"What's a mithchief maker?" Jack lisped, his eyes wide.

"Mischief, Mr. Big Ears." She reached forward and tickled him until he squirmed back down in his seat, then she turned to whisper to me. "He's really gone this time."

My mind wandered off into the fields all morning instead of staying in the classroom. At lunchtime, Becca and I sat across from the boys. "Confess," Becca ordered, pointing her finger at them.

Josh smiled, picked up a pea, and threw it at her.

Becca squealed and stood up, raising her milk carton.

"Knock it off," Drew said. "Both of you."

She stuck out her tongue at Josh. "Pea-brain."

Drew leaned forward, his eyes not quite reaching mine. "Sorry about your scarecrow, Sam." His face blushed. "We'll help you find him."

❖

Mr. Crumble was spraying over rust spots on his red tractor. He cocked his ear toward Becca as she asked for his help with the missing scarecrow. "Hmm. I'll take a looky-see in the apple orchard."

The rest of us searched the pumpkin patch. Jack tagged along.

Drew briefly touched my arm. "He's got to be here somewhere." My heart raced for a moment. I almost wished that we wouldn't find the scarecrow. Becca rolled her eyes.

As we walked back, Josh headed toward the port-a-toilets. Jack looked undecided then ran after him.

Drew leaned against my abandoned post. "Maybe you could make another one."

I flipped my hood up to hide my eyes. "Not by tomorrow."

Drew sighed. "Maybe—"

Jack's shrieks interrupted him. "Samantha!"

Josh and Jack stood over a water trough near the port-a-toilets. At the bottom, face down, was my scarecrow.

"Mr. Austin!" Becca cried.

Jack pointed at Josh. "He found him."

"You can thank me any time," Josh said, smiling.

"Yeah, right." Becca grabbed his arm. "You probably knew he was there the whole time."

Josh shook her off. "Whatever."

We reached into the frigid water. A scuffling sound came from within the hay bale maze to our right. We froze, holding our breath. "Maybe," Jack whispered, "it's the mithchief maker—"

"Quiet, Mr. Big Ears!" Becca whispered back.

Two cats darted out from the maze entrance.

"Just a bunch of creepy cats," Josh laughed.

We loosened our shoulders and dragged out the sodden body. He wasn't ruined, but he looked cold and miserable. The four of us carried him back to his spot while Jack ran behind, picking up pieces of straw. I refastened him to the post and straightened his head. "Do you think he'll dry out?"

"I don't know," Becca said. "Josh did a good number on him this time."

Josh poked her in the chest. "I was the one who found him, remember?"

She poked him back. "Yeah, pretty convenient."

"He'll dry fast with this wind blowing," Drew said. He looked up at the cloudy sky. "As long as it doesn't rain."

"Or snow," Becca added.

❁

After supper, Becca came over. As she scribbled math equations and made eraser marks, I stared out at the season's first snowflakes. After a while, Becca threw down her pencil. "We can't let them get away with this."

The image of my wet scarecrow trickled into my mind. "We don't even know they did it."

She snorted. "Are you kidding? Did you see Josh's face when he 'found' Mr. Austin? Don't be stupid. He and Drew are the ones that put him there."

I shook my head. "I don't think Drew would do that."

"Yeah? What about Mr. Austin's shirt? It has the same paint that's on their dumb doctor guy."

"Mr. Crumble was using red paint," I pointed out.

"Right. Mr. Crumble's out to sabotage your entry." She gripped my shoulders and squeezed hard. "It's a contest. Duh. Money's involved." Becca shook her head, then let go. She stuffed her homework into her backpack and stood up. "I'm not going to stand by and watch those boys enjoy their fun. Are you coming or not?"

I trudged behind Becca in the dark. Jack had wanted to come but it was almost bedtime. "And your curfew's in an hour," Dad reminded me.

We cut through the woods. Snow had begun to accumulate on the ground. On the zigzagged path, Becca's flashlight revealed several footprints.

"I don't believe it!" she screeched when we reached the empty post. Again my metal man had disappeared. "They're going to wish they'd never entered this contest." She stamped off in the direction of Drew and Josh's entry.

I kicked at the post in the dark. Stupid scarecrow. The judging was in less than twenty-four hours. The wind picked up, and my ears filled with the whispers of straw men and the shuffle of feet. I ran down the path, my heart pounding.

The restaurant windows cast a dim light over several of the closer entries, bouncing off the figures and creating eerie shadows. I darted across the lot to check behind the dumpster. Nothing. I hurried over to the water trough and looked in. No scarecrow.

Someone grabbed my arm. I stifled a scream. "The boys are sneaking around," Becca whispered. "C'mon. Follow me."

Becca peered through the dark. "They were just here."

The restaurant lights blinked off. Bells tinkled as Mrs. Crumble closed the front door.

"Oh, crap. I can't see anything now." Becca fumbled with her flashlight.

A light swept over us and the cornfield. "Howdy do out there!"

We dove to the ground.

"Hello?" Mr. Crumble called again.

"What's wrong?" Mrs. Crumble's voice was faint.

"Nothing, hon. Just thought I heard something."

We didn't move until they drove away. "You better go," Becca said, brushing snow off her jeans. "Meet me back here before the bus comes. I have the perfect plan of how to get those boys disqualified."

I burst through the door ten minutes late. "Sorry, Dad," I panted and then told him about my disappearing scarecrow.

"Still," Dad said, "I was worried. I know you want to win, Samantha, but a curfew is a curfew."

I turned toward my room, but Dad stopped me. "Drew came by. Said he needed to talk to you. It sounded important."

Drew answered on the first ring.

"We know you and Josh were there tonight," I said. "We saw your footprints, and Becca says she saw you."

"Sam, I know what you're thinking, but—"

"How could you, Drew?"

"I didn't do anything. I swear."

I clenched my jaw.

"Josh thought we should keep an eye on the scarecrows, just in case someone tried to mess around again. When we got there, yours was already missing." He paused. "Sam, did you hear me?

"We looked all over, then gave up. I wanted to tell you—I came straight to your house. But you were gone. Sam, you still there?"

"I got to go."

❋

I finished my cereal just as the doorbell rang.

"Samantha!" Jack yelled. "It's Drew and Josh."

Crap. I was supposed to be meeting Becca any minute.

Jack kept them busy while I combed my hair, brushed my teeth, and fumed. As I stomped down the stairs, I heard Jack's voice going a mile a minute. "…and my costume has a helmet and real shoulder pads."

"Hey, Sam," Drew said. "Can we talk?"

I grabbed my jacket and thrust my arms through the sleeves. "Jack," I said, "I'm going to meet Becca. I'll see you at the bus."

"I'll come with you." Jack reached for his shoes.

"Not this time, buddy. Sorry." I brushed past the boys and out into the cold air.

"Sam, please." Drew lumbered up to join me while Josh lagged behind, whipping a branch against tree trunks. "Why don't you believe me?" he asked, blocking my path. I plowed to his left.

Thwack, thwack, Josh continued his punishment.

Drew stepped in the same direction, forcing my face to almost collide into his chest. "I didn't mess with your scarecrow." He touched my shoulder but I shrugged him off.

"Then who did?" I blurted. "Who would be so mean to … to …" My voice broke and tears filled my eyes.

"Bus is almost here!" Josh's voice echoed through the trees. He ran back through the woods, the long branch in his hand tracing a path behind him.

As we walked in silence the rest of the way, Drew stole an occasional glance at my face. We entered the cornfield and spotted Becca with a tall figure next to her. She appeared slumped over. "Something's wrong," I said. We broke into a run.

Mr. Crumble towered over Becca, his eyes narrowed and his mouth turned down. "I'm sorry," she wailed. As soon as she saw me, she stood up. Her cheeks were splotched red and wet with tears. "Sam, it was a joke. They were all just stupid jokes." She raised her hands in surrender. "I, I didn't mean anything by it."

Mr. Austin's body lay spread out across two sawhorses. Drew and Josh's straw surgeon loomed over him, gripping a real saw. Red paint dripped from the blade and onto Mr. Austin's sliced throat. His head lay on the ground. Next to Becca's feet was a can of spray paint.

"Becca," I whispered. "Why?"

Mr. Crumble bent over and picked up the can. "I think we have ourselves a sore loser from last year." He straightened and handed it to Becca. "Whaddya say to that, young lady?"

Becca looked down and sniffled. "It just isn't fair. Everybody always wins but me."

Mr. Crumble cleared his throat. "First things first—an apology to all the contestants. Then, I think some afterschool clean-up chores." He turned toward me. "I'll explain everything to the Mrs., and we'll have the volunteers hold off on the judging. Sound good?"

I nodded.

Drew and I headed toward the restaurant to call our parents and explain why we had missed the bus. Becca trudged behind us, blowing her nose into a wad of tissue.

"I'm sorry," I said, peeking up at Drew. "I should've known better." I snuck a glance at Becca and then looked back at him. "You've always been a good friend." I stepped in front to block his path and turned to face him. With a half-smile and a deep breath, I offered him my trembling hand.

Release

Barbara Merritt Deese

In her deep-set eyes, golden with a black band, I saw intelligence and an unquenchable spirit. A little mystery too, since a Lakota man told me many Native Americans considered the red-tailed hawk to be a visionary and a messenger. Only the recipient of the Great Spirit's message, he'd said, will understand its meaning.

Someone had found the red-tail near Highway 169 and brought her to the Raptor Rehab of Minnesota. It was late afternoon on my second day volunteering there and I'd just finished cleaning the cages. I don't know what I'd expected to feel, but watching the vet ease back bloodied feathers to check her head and wing injuries, I saw not just a hawk, her beak open in mute helplessness—but also the formidable hunter she would become. She'd languished for two weeks, and then one day, when I offered her a mouse in the jaws of a forceps, she'd torn into it with gusto. She hasn't lost her appetite since.

"We don't name the rehab birds," my trainer had told me that first day. "It's not good to get too attached." Even without naming this hawk, I was conflicted about her being released into the wild. She was especially keen today, picking up on the mounting excitement of the occasion.

In Minnesota, early May, the weather was always iffy, and today was no exception. Scattered showers were in the forecast for the next three days, and an ominous cloud had taken up residence over the festivities. I was grateful for my heavy anorak. But in this lush preserve north of the Twin Cities, signs of spring were all around.

Families spilled from vans and cars. The Spring Release attracted people of all sorts. Mothers carried babies strapped to their chests or in backpacks. Wide-eyed kids pointed and ran toward the roped-off areas to see raptors up close, and bombarded the handlers with questions. Parents weren't afraid to let their children learn about both the beauty and brutality of nature.

I joined some people gathered around a bald eagle. A small boy picked at a scab on his knee and asked, "Why does the eagle have to kill bunnies?"

"Actually, he'd prefer fish, but when he can't catch any, he'll eat whatever he can find," the handler answered and drew the child's attention to the bird's powerful talons and hooked beak. He didn't question the boy about his own eating habits or suggest he might also eat dead animals. If you were a small rodent, I suppose this day was no cause for celebration, but it was really something to behold when a bird of prey made a kill. In the beginning, I hadn't been sure I could deal with the violence, but working with these birds had taught me something about survival.

"I can't believe I let you drag me out here for this!" The man's grating voice was all wrong in this bucolic setting. My guts did a familiar twist as he pressed past me in the crowd, a big man in a leather jacket with a nasty curl on his lip. "From now on I make the plans." He hurled the words over his shoulder. I followed their trajectory and saw the woman trudging behind him. She was hunched over, making her seem older than she must have been. Her flip-flops slap, slap, slapped against her dirty heels as she tried to keep pace with him. Her pallid face showed no indication that his words had struck their target, but I recognized the dead eyes and the gravity pulling her head into submission.

I squared my shoulders and remembered. For thirteen interminable years I'd been beaten down by belittling phrases that had damaged me more than if he'd used fists. It had taken me a long time and professional help to quit asking why I'd stayed with Cal so long. *Cognitive dissonance.* That was the term my therapist used to describe the craziness that had allowed me to believe Cal loved me, even as toxic words had fallen out of his mouth.

It was my therapist who had steered me to Raptor Rehab when I'd first left my husband. I'd gone grudgingly, taking two buses from the women's shelter to get there. After a brief training, I'd returned, eager to meet my first raptor. The red-tail had been in rough shape, but to be honest, I couldn't have told you which of us was more broken. Despite my trainer's caution that the bird did not view me as a friend, there was no denying the empathy I felt for the bedraggled creature.

The man bellowed above the crowd noise once more. "What kind of an idiot—?" That's all I heard. I repressed an urge to plant my fist in his face. Just last week, my therapist had reminded me I needed to resolve my anger issues.

The woman was obviously cold in a T-shirt and too-big jeans. The wind blew her hair back exposing purplish smudges on her neck. The man's legs kept moving, piston-like, but the woman was suddenly drawn to one of the roped-off areas where a young volunteer was explaining the habits of the Cooper's hawk. Leaning over the rope, the woman asked, "When will this bird be released?"

The volunteer scratched his beard with a heavily gloved hand and looked at the hawk's blood-red eyes. "This is one of our education ambassadors that has a permanent home at the Rehab. We'll be releasing a different Coop today."

"What about that one then, the one you're releasing? When she's out on her own, how will she survive?" the woman persisted.

He smiled. "The instinct is there. The Coop stays concealed and relies on complete surprise to catch food. Now, this one is just a teenager, and as anyone with teenagers knows, they can be aggressive, and a bit clumsy." He got a few chuckles from the crowd. "When it's the right time, she'll manage on her own," he assured her.

Leather Jacket doubled back like a heat-seeking missile, and I saw his expression. There was a time Cal could disarm me with a grin like that until I'd become acquainted with the anger it masked. I saw the woman brace herself for a blow that didn't come, at least not in the physical sense. He snorted and leaned down menacingly to say something in her ear. She stared straight ahead, not moving a muscle. I'd seen rabbits freeze like that when frightened.

"Let's go," Leather Jacket commanded. He took off again, confident she'd follow.

Just before she left, her eyes passed over the faces and stopped for a moment on mine. I watched her walk away, and a few seconds later, she threw me a wistful look. I considered running after her to invite her to my self-defense class.

When the time came, I took my place behind the makeshift stage. The birds to be released were hooded and wrapped in canvas. One of the veterinarians went to the microphone and recited a few facts about the sharp-shinned hawk. A volunteer uncovered the bird, lifted it into the air while clutching it by the ankles, and opened his hand. The bird took off in a graceful arc and found shelter in a nearby tree.

A juvenile bald eagle, always a crowd pleaser, was next, and as soon as he was free, he spread his magnificent wings to *ooohs* and *aaahs* and shutter clicks.

And then I saw my Raptor Rehab friend mounting the steps, cradling my red-tailed hawk like a huge feathered baby with talons and beak. The bird's eyes searched for me, or at least that's what I told myself. A breeze ruffled her white breast feathers. A few splats of rain fell on my folded arms. When my friend tilted the hawk back and gently propelled her forward and upward, I closed my eyes and all I heard was the soft slice of wings. By the time I looked again, she was soaring toward a large stand of trees. A ray of sunshine pierced the clouds as if showing her the way. She gained altitude and came to rest on a high, dead branch. We waited, but it looked like she was going to stick around for a while.

Soon the crowd began to disperse. We all pitched in to pack up the vans, but I wasn't ready to leave. I saw the uphill path leading toward the trees and started trudging up a narrow and crumbling trail along a sharp ridge. The red-tail was no longer on her high perch. I stopped to scan the treetops before I spied a dark shape in a lower branch, but without my binoculars I couldn't tell for sure if it was my hawk. When I tried to get closer, I stumbled on a tree root and realized I'd left the trail and was headed toward a sign that warned, Stay Away From Cliff Edges.

I heard a distant, mewling sound and looked up to see the man in the leather jacket coming toward me with the woman in tow, precariously close to the cliff's edge. Stopping in front of a sheer wall of rock that nearly blocked their way, he pushed her ahead of him. "Watch where you're going!" he barked. The treacherous path was suitable only for a mountain goat, but she pressed on in her flimsy flip-flops, stopping only when she'd rounded the outcropping. Her eyes were as hard as the stones that showered down the cliff below her.

He began to inch forward, all of his bluster gone now. His lips were pressed together in concentration. As soon as he'd gotten on the other side of the rock wall, he relaxed. "Well, what are you waiting for?" he said, rolling his wrist in a gesture to keep moving.

It all happened so fast. A blood-curdling shriek came from the trees, and we all looked up as a blur of wings and rusty tail feathers passed overhead. Leather Jacket cowered, took a step and staggered. Momentum drove him forward. Suddenly he was kicking up gravel and grabbing air as he plunged over the edge.

I rushed from my shadowed hiding place, startling the woman, who grabbed me and held on. Then together we clutched an overhanging branch and looked down. He lay motionless on a boulder-strewn ledge several yards below, with one arm folded under him and his head tilted sharply against his shoulder.

We stepped back. I reached in my pocket for my phone, pulled it out and dialed 911. "A man just fell over the cliff. I think his neck is broken," I said, hearing the tremor in my voice.

The woman began to shiver uncontrollably. We sat together on a fallen tree and waited for help. I saw again the bruises on her neck and put my arm around her. "Are you going to be okay?" I asked.

"Yes, I think so," she finally answered. She lifted her head high and faced me squarely. The deadness I'd seen in her eyes was gone, replaced by the astonishment of someone waking to realize it had all been a bad dream.

"It was an accident," I said, marveling at how easily the lie was born. Even though it will be a heavy burden, I will never reveal her secret. After seeing the sudden realization on her face that she'd been given a chance at freedom, how could I? In that split second, I'd known what she was going to do, and I'd rooted for her as her leg had shot out in a simple reflex, catching him square on his ankle and sending him to his death.

I heard the messenger's rasping scream and searched for her. She shrieked again, and I saw her eyes, golden with a black band, peering at me through the foliage. We stared at each other for several seconds. Then, with a few quick flaps of her wings, she was airborne. I watched as she rose on a current of air and disappeared.

Sketches For Cinco

Sheyna Galyan

"*¡Hola!*" I called to the passersby as they meandered through Parque Castillo. "Sketches for Cinco!"

A young Latino family with a chubby-cheeked toddler and two school-age girls stopped in front of my art booth at the Cinco de Mayo Festival on St. Paul's West Side to look at my sign offering a pencil sketch for five dollars. I smiled and tucked some loose hair behind my ear. I'd been told this makes me look harmless and friendly.

"*Solamente cinco dolares*," I said, using the rest of the Spanish I knew. "I can sketch your whole family. It only takes a few minutes."

The mom hesitated, then shook her head with an apologetic smile. "The parade is about to start. We want to get good seats." They continued toward Cesar Chavez Street.

I sat down in the folding chair next to my easel. I'd sold two paintings, one on silk and one on glass, since the festival started. While that covered my booth fee, it wasn't going to pay the looming utility bills.

I heard a band starting to play in the distance and told myself I might as well relax; the parade was one of the most popular parts of the festival. Most of the other vendors had their wares spread out over colorful blankets on the ground. I was one of the few who had brought a canopy, mostly to protect my art from sun or rain—or the remote possibility of snow—depending on Minnesota's fickle weather. The day's overcast sky made me grateful for my forethought.

The parade was underway and I saw a number of St. Paul police officers around, no doubt because the governor, the mayor, and the police chief were all in the parade. Along with Ronald McDonald. I wondered briefly if they came as a set.

I was just getting up from my seat, hoping to see the parade from my spot in the center of the park's large open area, when something crashed into my easel and knocked me over. I scrambled to my feet, my heart pounding.

"Hide me!" pleaded the young man who had run into my easel. "Hide me! They're going to kill me!"

"Who?" I asked, looking around. "There are police here. I'll call them."

"No!" He looked around my booth in an apparent panic, then crawled behind the large painting I had propped up against a card table.

"Wait! You can't—" I stopped when I realized what might be happening. The young man was dressed in an oversized brown hoodie and baggy jeans. The top of a tattoo that looked like an Old English "B" peeked out above his collar, dark against his mocha skin. He was younger than I'd first thought, barely a teenager, but I knew gangs recruited young. I glanced back at Cesar Chavez Street. The cops had moved on.

I had a cell phone in my bag, in the back corner of the booth with my art supplies, but I couldn't get to it without going past the kid under my table. And I didn't know if I could trust him.

I set my easel back upright, trying to slow my breathing. Why was there never a cop around when you wanted one? Across the park, I saw a group of teens sauntering past the vendors, all dressed in varying shades of blue. One of them, a tall, skinny Latino, wore a blue basketball jersey with the number thirteen in white, and had a blue bandana tied around his head. He was calling out to others in a voice that was both angry and defiant.

I've lived on the West Side a long time, which is why I was eligible to sell my art at Cinco, despite being fish-belly white and horribly deficient in Spanish. My parents lived down on the Flats when it was mostly an immigrant Jewish community, before it had become District Del Sol.

One thing I tried to pay attention to was the infiltration of gangs. I didn't know the language or understand the graffiti, but I knew colors when I saw them. And I also knew that the City of St. Paul had recently banned gang colors—and some gang members—from Cinco.

No question, it was time to get my cell phone. But as I started toward the back of the booth, the kid scrambled out from under the table and raced past me, narrowly missing my easel, and ran for the trees in the northwest corner of the park. I grabbed my bag, found my phone, and tapped in 9-1-1.

"Nine one one, what is your emergency?"

I looked across the park where the teens in blue had been. There was no sign of them. "I'm at the Cinco de Mayo festival in St. Paul, in Parque

Castillo with the vendors. I saw some gang members here; they might be chasing someone."

"Okay, ma'am. I'll send an officer to your location."

Ninety seconds later, I saw an officer enter the park from Cesar Chavez, visually scanning the vendors. I waved and caught his attention.

"I'm Sergeant Pomelo," he said when he reached my booth. He was tall and stocky, and carried himself with casual ease. He had a bald head and the lines on his face told me he laughed a lot. "Are you the one who called?"

I nodded. "A young teen crashed into my booth a few minutes ago, saying he had to hide because *they*," I emphasized the word with air quotes, "were going to kill him. Then I saw a bunch of teens over there," I pointed to the end of the park nearest the Wellstone Center, "who were all in blue, looking very gang-ish. The one in charge had a blue bandana and a number thirteen jersey. The kid ran off toward the trees right before I called."

Sergeant Pomelo frowned, muscles pulling against his laugh lines. "Sureño Thirteens. They've been banned from this event. Could you tell if the young teen was part of the same gang?"

"No," I said, shaking my head. "He seemed pretty scared of them. He was wearing a brown hoodie."

"Can you describe him? His face?"

I pointed to my easel. "I can do better than that." I grabbed a couple of pencils and began sketching the kid. I wanted to make it fast, so I didn't do the kind of shading and nuance I'd usually put into a sketch, but I took the time to pencil in the tattoo. I tore the page off my drawing pad and handed it to him.

"Excellent," he said. "I'll go compare this to the gang book. See if he's anyone we know."

"Gang book?"

"Yeah, we've got a book—a binder—with photos and info on all the known gang members in St. Paul. If he's in there, we'll know who he is, where he lives, what he ate for breakfast." He reached into his breast pocket and pulled out a business card. "May I?" he indicated my pencil. I handed it to him and he scribbled something on the card. "Here's my card and my direct cell number. If you see them here again, call me. Okay?"

"Sure." I took the card and pencil from him. The thought that I should program his cell number into my speed dial flashed through my brain, but I was distracted by another family who were talking to each other appreciatively about my art pieces and pointing at my Sketches for Cinco sign. Sergeant Pomelo headed back toward Cesar Chavez with the sketch I'd drawn of the young man.

"Can you draw our kids all together, and then each one separate?" the mother asked.

I smiled and tucked my hair. "I sure can."

❀

After the parade ended, the stream of customers was steady. I even had a waiting line for a bit. Some of the women were dressed in traditional Mexican dresses with brightly colored full skirts and embroidered blouses; their hair was tied back and adorned with flowers. Two teenage girls wore matching white dresses with intricately embroidered peacocks on the bodice and skirt. I decided to switch to colored pencils for their sketches.

I was in the middle of a sketch of a three-generation family—grandfather, father, and very wiggly infant son—trying to hurry while the mom waited to one side and kept pointedly checking her watch, when there was a loud BANG nearby. Everyone froze and looked around for evidence of an exploding device nearby or someone with a gun. After that moment of stunned paralysis, the mom grabbed her baby, shouted "¡Vamanos!" and took off in the opposite direction from the explosion.

The news spread quickly across the vendor area: the explosion was a car backfire from the nearby lowrider car show. We all breathed a sigh of relief, but the event had broken the festival mood. The people who had been waiting for a sketch ventured elsewhere.

To stretch my legs and relieve the tension in my shoulders I took a stroll outside my booth. Movement in the trees edging the park caught my eye, and I saw the kid in the brown hoodie again as he was being pushed around by the gang in blue that had been looking for him earlier. I watched the shoving for a second—*any chance it was friendly?*—until the guy in the jersey punched the kid in the stomach. The kid dropped to the ground.

I went running toward them, not realizing until I was halfway there that I had no clue what I was going to do. I had my cell phone in my pocket, but the kid didn't have time for me to stop and dial Sergeant's

Pomelo's number. The only other thing I was armed with was a pencil, tucked in my back pocket. What was I going to do, take on a known street gang with a 5B Derwent?

"Hey!" I yelled as I approached the group of boys. They were taking turns taunting the kid who was now lying on the ground. "Stop!"

Jersey Thirteen turned and looked at me with eyes so cold that I immediately regretted my intrusion. I stopped in the grass a few feet away, certain he was going to pull out a gun and shoot me. My heart was pounding and there was a rushing noise in my ears.

"This ain't none of your business," Jersey Thirteen said roughly.

"Well, it kind of is. He," I pointed to the kid on the ground, "asked for my help earlier."

"Oh, and you gonna give it to him, bitch?"

I tried to get my breathing under control. "Um. My name is Tali, not bitch. And I'd really prefer it if you didn't do any more harm to him."

"You'd *prefer* it?" Jersey Thirteen said with a swagger.

"Yes." I nodded, holding eye contact with him even though it was the scariest thing I'd ever done. "Please."

"Oooh," several of the other guys said, slapping each other and mimicking me. "She said *pleeease*."

"What's your name?" I asked Jersey Thirteen.

"Why you wanna know my name?"

I tucked my hair and tried a smile. "Because you're a person. And every person has a name."

He broke our eye contact first, then looked at the ground, shaking his head. "Shit." He swung around and pointed at me, giving me a second mini heart attack. "No, that's not my name. My *eses* call me T-Rex."

"What about your real name? For those who aren't your *eses*?"

"Whadda you care?" he demanded, and I was pretty sure I heard pleading beneath the bravado. Then in a softer tone he said, "Tomás."

A couple of the other guys started to jeer at that, and then must have thought better of it.

"Tomás," I said, "why do you want to hurt this kid?"

"His *hermano*—his brother—is BFL. And he's in our territory, trying to take what's ours."

"He got out!" the kid pleaded. "The police, they caught him and he got out so he wouldn't go to jail. He works for them now, at Boys and Girls Club."

"*¿Su hermano trabaja para la policía?*"

"*Sí.* He's no threat to you. Only to BFL."

"What's BFL?" I asked.

"Don't you know nothing, *chica*?" Tomás asked. "BFL is Brown For Life."

"So can you let him go, Tomás? Please?"

"*Esta vez,*" Tomás finally said. He made a motion to the others in blue. "Come on." They left and went further into the trees, toward Robert Street.

The kid got to his feet. "Thanks. You're not like most people. Nobody talks to him like that."

I took a long, shaky breath. "Maybe if more people treated him like a human being, he wouldn't need to be in a gang." I studied the boy for a minute. What's your name?"

"Ian."

"*Ian?*"

"My dad's Irish."

"Okay, Ian. I called the police when you ran from my booth because I thought you were in trouble. They're looking for you. I'm going to call them back to tell them you're okay. Will you go back with me to my booth?"

He nodded. I pulled Sergeant Pomelo's card from my pocket and tapped the number into my phone. We started walking slowly back to the vendor area.

"Pomelo," the sergeant answered.

"Hi, it's Tali, in the vendor area? I found the kid who was running. He's okay."

"Good. I want to come talk to him. Are you in your booth?"

"We're on our way."

❁

"Ian, my man," Sergeant Pomelo said as he approached us. He high-fived Ian, and then offered his hand for me to shake. As I took it, he said, "We ID'd him right away in the book, but we were looking more to the east and south. Figured that's where we'd find him, maybe along Prescott." He turned to Ian. "Where were you?"

"T-Rex and his guys grabbed me." He motioned to me. "She came running and talked T-Rex into letting me go. Even got him to tell her his name is Tomás."

Pomelo looked at me the way I must have looked at Ian when he told me his name. "Really? Are you looking for a job?"

"I'd rather draw," I said, feeling embarrassed.

"Good. Because that was, pardon my expression, fantastically stupid. You should have called me. What if those gang members were armed?"

"I don't know." I didn't tell him about my pencil weapon.

Pomelo sighed. "Well-meaning citizens playing hero are going to be the death of me yet."

"I'm sorry." I remembered something. "Ian, you said not to call the police when you first hid in my booth. If your brother works for them, why not call?"

"I was afraid the gang would start shooting."

"But Tomás didn't have a gun," I said.

"Yes he did. In his waistband under his jersey. I saw the outline from the back."

"T-Rex and his gang," Pomelo said slowly, "are suspected in several shootings, including firing at a police officer."

"And I just ran up and started talking to him?" I asked. My knees felt unsteady. I moved over to my chair and sat down before I fainted.

"You did say please," Ian pointed out. "And no offense, but you look pretty harmless."

I smiled faintly and tucked my hair. "So I've been told."

Best of the Fest

Mickie Turk

Your eyelids fling open and cement your eyelashes to the top of your brow bone. Liquid oozes down your arms. You smell copper. Blood. Without looking, you run a finger across the wetness and taste it. Salty. *Not* blood. You're drenched in sweat from head to toe. You've had the nightmare again.

You want to shake it off. But blinking is like peeling membranes from your skull, and moving limbs, cramped from fighting monsters in the night, hurts like hell. Finally, you draw on supernatural energy and roll over onto your side and sit up. You pull the handle of the small drawer on the nightstand and reach in. The letter makes it into your balled-up fist. You've made copies of the original and placed them all over the house. And the car. You wanted to make sure that the letter was real. And stayed real.

You read it for the last time.

Dear Ava,

Forty-three years have passed, but not a day has gone by without my thinking of that glorious afternoon we spent together. You were only twelve years old.

For all my travels and accomplishments, I have never felt so much pure and simple joy as on the day that you walked into my life. Your face, your arms, and legs, those images—live on in my memory. You haunt me.

Back then it was the age of innocence—pure and pristine. I want it back. You can give it back to me.

You want it too, don't you?

The V.I.P. pass will get you into any film at the festival, but just stick to the documentary features. I look the same. And I'd recognize you anywhere because I've watched over you since the summer of 1965.

FIND ME.

The laminated festival pass for the Minneapolis St. Paul International Film Festival (MSPIFF) has a photo of you on the front. He must have pulled it off Google Images or one of your personal websites. You'd thought about cutting your hair, wearing a hat or wig, but decided against it because he's right. Like him, you've been waiting forever for this.

One second you're terrified. The next exhilarated. And then another feeling surfaces. Anxiety. Maybe the letter was a joke sent by an anonymous sadist and only approximated the toxic events of that summer. You ponder the statistical probability of its randomness.

Wait. Whoever sent the letter knows what you were called before and the year it happened. And that same person bought you a four-hundred-dollar festival pass. It has to be him. But what if you don't spot him? What if he'd already attended one of the other documentaries and you missed him? Maybe he was at one of the after-parties. You could have walked right by while he was working the wine bar or noshing at a crowded hors d'oeuvres table.

Once a year, cinephiles crowd into MSPIFF to watch an endless parade of features and shorts that showcase the finest in cutting-edge artistry and storytelling. You've watched twenty-two documentaries in eighteen days. The last three documentaries play today, and you have to eliminate one because two of the films run at the same time. It's not difficult to pass up *When Russia Meows*. A film about the yearly Vladivostok cat show and competition is simply too sweet. Incredibly, the remaining two are dramatic case histories of torture, victims, and their abusers. He has to be at one of them. It's his *thing*.

As you fold the letter in two, the entire reel of your life spools backwards until it stops at the front steps of your childhood home.

❀

The air is summer-steamy and the sun so bright, it has completely bleached the sky of all its color. You can just make out the click clacking of your best friend's thong sandals as she hurries down the sidewalk toward you.

"Did you see him yesterday? Did you?" she asks. Her face is flushed from the heat as much as the anticipation of what your answer might be.

"The other boys were on the porch, but not him," you say.

"You think he's gone? Already? Back to St. Paul?" She shakes her head. "He could've been in the back yard or getting something to eat in the kitchen."

Your insides make gurgling sounds and your heart beats tiny hammers inside your ears. You want him to still be there. Not gone. Not all the way to St. Paul. Not when you live in Minneapolis.

"Let's take the long way to the park. We can go by the house again."

You walk barefoot across hot sidewalks and even hotter macadam intersections where cars are rarely seen in the mid-morning. The smell of burning tar from nearby smokestacks competes with freshly cut grass as you pass Mr. Sherman's manicured lawn. When you and your friend loop around the western end of the park, the two-story moves into view. Hard to miss with its red-brick, asphalt-shingle siding. The older boys are sitting on the porch handrail, smoking. One of the gingerbread balusters is cracked off at the bottom. The visitor, who you think looks just like Herman Hermits' front man, Peter Noone, stands with one arm over his head, pulling on a strand of long, curly blonde hair. He's even cuter than the singer. He's staring straight at you and he's smiling.

"He likes you Ava. He can't stop looking at you," she whispers.

Now you're flying into the park like you have wings. And your best friend is right behind you. Panting, you both land on black rubber-seated swings and chortle. When you settle down, you discuss every single detail of what just transpired between the boy and you. Conclusion: the Peter Noone look-alike with china blue eyes—yes, indeed—has a crush on you. You think you will die from happiness.

Your best friend says she has to go home, but she's going to walk a different way. She's supposed to go to grandma's house to pick up a jar of homemade pickles for her dad. But you go back the way you came. One more time by the house. You're still across the street when you notice he's sitting by himself on the handrail. He motions for you to come over.

❧

There are many benefits to owning a VIP festival pass. Not only will it get you into as many films as you want, including next week's audience choice awards, The Best of the Fest, but most of the parties are free, and you're allowed—even encouraged—to go to the head of the line before each film. They always call the festival pass owners first—sometimes to the chagrin of the people standing directly behind you, who've been waiting for thirty minutes or longer.

You sit down in your usual spot: two thirds back in the middle of the theater. This way you can turn your head easily to watch filmgoers stream in on both sides. They're slow at first, but very quickly the masses begin to descend down the aisles like schools of fish. You keep careful track of each male. You've become a trained detective. First, you know he'll be in his early sixties and he'll come alone. Second, you'll be able to glimpse his china blue eyes even in the dark.

You reach into your handbag and begin the ritual. You realize that your tin of lemon-flavored hard candy is almost empty, but you root around until you find one and plop it in your mouth. You suck on the candy, lean back, and cross your arms. As the lights dim, a volunteer runs breathlessly to the front and gives a short description of the film. You look at the program guide: director in attendance. There will be a Q & A afterwards. The short video that precedes every film begins, followed by images of the sponsors' logos. You look around you. He's not here. There are only two men in their sixties who sit alone. One is African-American and the other you recognize as one of the ushers. Your earlier adrenaline rush fades and turns into exhaustion. You fall asleep. When you wake up, you take out another piece of candy and suck on it. This time it helps you stay awake until the end. But you're watching another kind of film.

❂

"Want to come up to my room? I have a TV," he yells.

You cross the street fighting a stream of litter that swims against the curb. The wind picks up, lifting and propelling the detritus forward. Cigarette butts, candy wrappers, and the front page of today's morning paper skitter away just in time for you to jump up onto the grassy boulevard. On the porch steps you look up and smile shyly. Of course you're going to get grounded for the rest of the summer. Who cares, he has a TV.

There's a strong odor in the house. Earlier, somebody had been cooking with onions. You notice the sink. It's piled high with dirty dishes. Where is everyone?

"My aunt and uncle and cousins went down to the river to fish. They won't be back until dark," he explains.

You walk up the stairs and he offers you the only chair in his room while he perches on the edge of the bed. He asks you what school you'll be going to in September. Then he wants to know how well you know his older cousins.

"I don't talk to them. I just see them playing ball in the park," you answer. He nods thoughtfully.

You look around for a TV. There isn't one.

❀

You have time before the next film and go outside to one of the nearby patio restaurants. In the gloaming, Minneapolis feels like Victorian Europe. The street is lined with hundred-and-fifty-year-old cobblestones, and the brick and colonnaded limestone buildings are the oldest masonry structures in the city. In front of you, the Mississippi River shimmers with reflections from Downtown West's skyscrapers and Downtown East's historic mill district. As the sun lowers to say goodnight, cotton-candy clouds float across the orange sky. You don't see any of it because the past ambushes you again.

❀

"It's better to pretend than to really watch TV," he says. "We can write the stories and be movie stars inside our own television show."

You like to pretend and you write stories too. But his story is not nice.

"You can be the pretty lady who's home alone, and I can be the bad guy who breaks into her apartment," he says.

You agree because you're certain that if this cute boy can play the bad guy, it's probably just a disguise for the hero underneath. What do you know? All the things you've learned to expect from life have come out of the pages of *TEEN* magazine.

He asks if the gag over your mouth is too tight.

"No."

He cinches it tighter.

"Do you care if I tie your hands behind you? It has to look real, you know."

I have to go home right now, you think. But you never struggle against the rope he twines around your wrists. Your muscles are frozen solid with fear.

When he comes around to stand in front of you, he's holding a Mason jar. He sets it down on the floor and unscrews the cover. He pours out the contents. You close your eyes and hear soft tinkling. A symphony of tiny chimes.

"Don't worry," he says.

The tears fall slowly down your cheek and dribble off your chin, soaking into your shirt collar.

When he's finished, he hurries to the bathroom and shuts the door. He stays in there a long time. In the distance you can make out a fan and its intermittent whirring and hissing. Something's in the blades. Caught just like you, you think. At least *it's* making a racket.

When he comes back he unties you, loosens the gag, and leaves the room. When the screen door slams downstairs, you lower your eyes and assess the damage.

Almost imperceptible pools of blood form crooked roadways up and down your arms and legs. A few sewing pins are still stuck in the skin near your ankles. As you pull them out, you stare at the floor. You guess he's used a hundred of them. Under the bathtub faucet your skin runs clear after a few minutes, and most of the wounds seal up. You stick toilet paper on a couple stubborn bleeders and begin the walk home. Your parents are outside working in the vegetable garden and don't notice your slinking in through the side door. You run up to your room and stay there until morning.

❁

You've been trying to watch the last documentary, but you've lost the thread. Somewhere in a remote Eastern European village there'd been a parade, followed by demonstrations. Then masked men ran out and attacked the girls who came to march without boyfriends. No one stopped them; no one came to rescue the victims. The film ends much like it started, with demonstrations.

You're disconsolate. He didn't show. As you get up to leave, your candy tin falls out of your handbag and drumrolls down the slanted floor. *Figures.* You lean over and grab it. When you straighten, you see him. Blonde hair, china blue eyes. Up on the screen his figure is superimposed over the credits. Looking fit in khaki shirt, cargo pants, and safari hat, he's glad-handing enthusiastic university students who say they love the film and thank him for making it. Then you remember: *Director In Attendance.*

Peter Noone's doppelganger's china blue eyes find yours as he strides down the aisle. The Q & A is short tonight, fifteen minutes. Afterwards, you ride the carpet of humanity outdoors. He's on the sidewalk, running. Now he's sliding his finger over the fingerprint scanner of his late model German sports car. Behind him, your made-in-America four-door looks conspicuously dated.

You pull out when he does and follow him for ten minutes. When he turns into the Dairy King on University Avenue, you do too. He gets out of the car and goes inside. You wait and take a snapshot of your surroundings. Your two cars are the only ones in the customer parking lot. When you walk around to the other side of the building, you see a small truck—one of the employee's vehicles, you guess.

You peer inside the windows and discern only two people working. One at the counter and another making the food. Both male.

You stand in line while he sits in a booth sipping a soft drink. He's texting as you order. Your phone chirps.

You found me.

I almost gave up.

Thoughts?

Meet me in the bathroom.

Which one?

You push open the women's door and he follows. You set your drink on top of the paper towel dispenser and close the door tightly. Then you lock it. There's a little bench by the changing table and you sit down. He leans against one of the sinks, arms folded.

"Aren't you thrilled you came?" he asks.

You nod. "But why did you wait until the last millisecond to show?"

"I wanted to gage your level of commitment."

"Did I pass?" you ask.

"Can you feel it? Are you as excited as I am? Except for that other time, this is the closest I will ever come to real happiness. Why don't we leave right now? We can go in my car. I still have a place in St. Paul."

In the harsh bathroom light the face still looks like young Peter Noone's, but it's put together with all the wrong stuff. First you notice his eyes are preternaturally blue. Contacts. And the rosebud mouth, once so sweet and soft on a teenaged boy, now looks like it owes its existence to a red lip liner. The blonde curls are actually white. Purple spidery veins crease the small nose. Yellow teeth grin dementedly at you. He's a smoker and a drinker.

"I could report you. I could tell the police what you did to me."

"Really, seriously? He arches an eyebrow in disappointment. "Who would believe you?"

"I'm supposed to grab a late dinner with a friend," you finally manage.

"Oh, with your *boy*friend, I suppose. Call him, tell him something came up and that you'll see him later."

"Okay." But you watch him a while longer. Big round eyes and an overwrought mouth sit awkwardly on the planes of a crumbling skull. The reddish-brown skin—he's probably installed a tanning bed in his house—appears puckered and drawn, much like an over-ripened sweet potato. He's too old to look that young. He reminds you of a ventriloquist's dummy.

You reach into your handbag as if to take out your cell phone. Instead, you smile broadly and stare inside. You're taking too long and he can't help himself. He pushes off the sink and pokes his nose unselfconsciously inside your handbag. That's when you straighten, turn your cheek, and pull the tab to release the anesthetic vapor. Chloroform. He'll be out for as long as it takes.

You grab the candy tin and lay it on your lap. You unscrew the top and peel off the quilted paper cushion to expose the bottom layer. For the first time since receiving the letter, you relax.

They're still there. All lying at different angles but winking happily at you. Long, glittering slivers posed at attention, waiting to do their job. Exactly one hundred brand new sewing pins.

You've finished and reach for the door handle. That's when a small doubt creases your consciousness. When the torturer wakes up, he could report you. Tell the police what you did to him. Just as quickly, the thought vanishes into orbit because, please … *Who would believe him?*

Looney Daze

Cheryl Ullyot

Del Gustafson was leaving Canterbury racetrack contemplating how he'd pay off his mounting gambling debts when the perfect solution presented itself.

Across the parking lot a group of middle-aged women were gathered in a circle, clapping and cheering. Curious, he sauntered over.

"What's happening?" he asked a petite blonde cradling a dachshund. She was fifty-ish and nice looking. She reminded him of an old girlfriend.

"The wiener dog races. Anthony here won his heat so he made the finals."

Her friends smiled and nodded.

"Good luck, Anthony," Del said as he patted the pup's head. Anthony chomped down on his finger. "Ouch!" he cried, shaking his hand.

"Sorry," said the blonde. "He's just excited. Aren't you, my wittow twoublemaker?"

A voice over the loudspeaker called for the finalists.

"Wish us luck," said the blonde.

As Del was leaving he overheard the other women talking.

"Isn't Myrna a doll?" remarked the woman in the straw hat. "It's so cute the way she dotes on that dog. He's her whole world."

"It's a shame she can't find a nice man," said another. "Hasn't Leonard been dead for over two years?"

"Three," said the straw-hatted woman. "She tried Internet dating with no luck. Myrna is so trusting—and has to be careful. Especially with all her money."

Del followed nonchalantly, keeping his distance, as they walked towards the racetrack.

"You'd never know she has money the way she lives. Leonard was very frugal. Myrna must have fainted when she found out he'd left her five million. She still hasn't gotten used to being rich."

Del smiled as an idea crested.

A consummate ladies' man and opportunist, Del was a sixty-five-year-old widower, trim, well spoken, and with expensive tastes. He often told his dates that he was independently wealthy; he would have been quite a catch if he'd been telling the truth.

Myrna reappeared with Anthony under her arm, waving a blue ribbon in her hand.

Del chased after her. "Congratulations!" he shouted. "Your dog won!"

"Yes, he was sensational. Weren't you, my tweet wittow winner?"

Del winced. He loathed women who spoke in baby talk. Still there was the five million dollar motivation.

"Do you mind if I see the little fellow one more time?" he asked. "He reminds me of a dog I had as a child. My parents gave him away because we were poor and couldn't afford to keep him." Del's eyes filled with tears.

"That's awful!" Myrna said," I couldn't live if someone gave my pwescious wittow Anthony away."

By the end of their conversation, Del and Myrna had a date.

Del called his bookie to assure him he'd be getting his money soon.

"That's good," Al said." I can't wait much longer. What's up, anyhow? Did you charm some rich widow or something?"

❁

Del pulled up to Myrna's small ranch-style house in Richfield. A 1999 Toyota sat in the driveway.

If I inherited five mil, the first thing I'd do is move out of this dump and buy a BMW. Once we're married, I'll insist Myrna do just that, he thought.

Myrna's husband, Leonard, had been a CPA. The way it sounded, the guy did nothing but work. Their entertainment amounted to watching *Wheel of Fortune* every night, and occasionally dining at Olive Garden.

"Len loved the endless salad bowl and breadsticks," Myrna had said.

Del would need to introduce Myrna to the finer things in life—at her expense, of course. He told her his money was temporarily tied up in a project in Costa Rica. *As long as I pamper the mutt, I'll have her eating out of my hand,* he schemed. He showered Anthony with doggie toys and treats.

After a month, Del was ready to pop the question. "Dearest, I know it's only been a few weeks, but they have been the happiest of my life. I hope you feel the same."

He leaned in for a kiss. Anthony jumped into Myrna's lap and growled.

"Wooks wike wittow Anthony wants some woving too," she said, pushing him into Del's face. Anthony bit his nose.

"Dammit!" Del shouted, about to whack Anthony off the couch. Myrna stiffened, horrified.

"Dammit, wittow Anthony sure is a wittow character," he chuckled, catching himself. He quickly lowered his hand and wiped the blood off his nose instead. "Marry me Myrna. At our age why wait?" he said, getting down on one knee.

"Oh, Del! This is so sudden. I don't know what to say. I must admit that it has been lonely without Leonard. I know you love Anthony as much as I do, but after losing someone you've loved, it's difficult to trust again."

"Myrna, I know exactly how you feel. You see, my wife died in a tragic accident."

Myrna gasped. "How?"

"Drowned," he replied, choking up. "But even after five years it's too hard for me to talk about."

"My poor lambie," she said, hugging his head to her bosom.

"I wanted to surprise you with an engagement ring, but I noticed you don't wear much jewelry. Not that you need to. Your natural beauty outshines any gems I could buy you."

Myrna blushed.

Anthony barked, and Myrna dropped Del's head like a rotten melon.

"Potty time," she said, then jumped up and grabbed Anthony's leash.

"Don't worry about an engagement ring," she said. "I don't need any jewelry. Leonard was a frugal man, but the one thing he splurged on was expensive jewelry for me every year on my birthday. Nice, but I never wear any of it. A little too flashy for my taste. Besides, I'd hate to lose something that cost so much, so I just keep it in my bedroom dresser drawer." She stood up. "I'm taking Anthony around the block. Will you be okay alone for a few minutes?"

Del nodded.

Once she'd left, Del raced into Myrna's bedroom and rifled through her drawers.

"Thank you Leonard," he said, looking skyward as he slipped a diamond tennis bracelet into his pocket. Since gold was at an all-time high, he grabbed a gold necklace as well.

When Myrna returned, she said, "I do trust you and I accept your proposal, dear Del."

❀

A few days later Myrna called Del. "Anthony is scheduled to compete in the National Wiener Dog Races at the Looney Daze Festival in Vergas. Like to join us? We could discuss our wedding plans."

"Love to," Del said and rolled his eyes.

Another wiener dog race. Would that be his life from now on? No, not for long.

❀

It was a four-hour drive to Vergas, Minnesota, a resort town close to the North Dakota border. Four hours in the car listening to Myrna's incessant baby talk. Del might as well be marrying Tweetie Bird. And talk about cheap. She made Leonard look like a spendthrift.

He'd kept himself busy thinking how his life would be after Myrna was out of the picture. He'd persuade her to take out an insurance policy, and then he'd have to kill her of course. He had no problem killing women. He'd done that on a couple of occasions before. His last wife had died from drowning in the bathtub. It wasn't an accident, but that's what the coroner had decided, so who was he to argue?

He was already planning Myrna's funeral. He'd seen a suit in Brooks Brothers that would be perfect for the occasion.

And Anthony would have to go as well, of course.

Myrna read from the festival schedule. "There's the Miss Vergas Pageant, a biscuits and gravy breakfast, a fishing tournament, then of course the hot laps and the races," she rambled on. He ignored her, focusing on where he could hock her diamond bracelet.

Entering Vergas, they'd passed the world's largest loon: a fifteen-foot-high statue on Long Lake. Del had expected to stay at one of the beautiful resorts in the area and hoped Myrna had rented a lakeside cabin. Instead, she directed him to pull off the highway onto a gravel parking lot. The only way to distinguish the line of rooms from storage units was a neon sign that read 'Motel.' Behind the motel was an open field with woods beyond.

"I never believed in paying a lot for hotel rooms," she said. "I did get us separate rooms, though. I don't think it's proper to stay together before we're married."

Thank God, Del thought. He had brought his laptop along and planned on doing some online gambling.

"And wemember, we need to get Anthony wested for the big wace."

God, I could kill her now. Del ripped the bandage off his nose.

Once settled, they drove into town. The place was bustling, although most of the events would start the next day. Myrna wanted to buy a T-shirt she'd seen in one of the shops. Del had told her to meet him in Billy's Corner bar. He could hardly wait to order a drink.

"You from the cities?" asked the old timer on the barstool next to him.

"Yeah," Del said.

"Where ya stayin'?"

"The motel on the Vergas trails."

The old timer raised an eyebrow. "Heard of the Hairy Man?"

"The what?"

"The Hairy Man—the famous legend."

"You mean Bigfoot?" Del laughed and motioned to the bartender for another scotch.

"Naw," the codger said. "The Hairy Man. Lives back in the woods, behind your motel. He's famous up here. They even did a show on him. Ever seen *Haunted Highway* on the Syfy channel?"

"Nope."

"Lotta people seen him. Years ago a coupla kids said he jumped on the hood of their car and dented it. Said he was seven or eight feet tall, with hair all over his body."

"Are you sure they weren't on LSD?"

"Some gals seen him too. He chased 'em with a hatchet."

Myrna walked into the bar wearing a T-shirt that read 'Wienies and Martinis.'

Beyond cheesy. But at least it wasn't a loon appliqué.

"Look, I bought a loon sweatshirt for you," she said and handed him a bag.

"What were you two talking about?" Myrna asked, as they drove to the motel.

"The old geezer said something about a demented hairy man living in the woods behind our motel. I think he was drunk."

"Don't wuwy," Myrna told Anthony. "Del will pwotect us from that bad ole haiwy man."

Del cringed.

❀

The next morning Del was outside on his cell phone. "Al, I need more time. I'm up in Vergas, but I'll get some cash to you on Monday."

"I'm tired of your excuses Del. I may have to drive up there and explain things to you."

"Look Al, I'm good for it, I swear. I'm about to marry this woman who's loaded."

"Is she generous?"

"Doesn't matter, she's not going to be around that much longer."

"Planning on running a bubble bath for her?"

"Let's just say her days are numbered."

"Make it soon."

Del held the diamond bracelet up to the sunlight and wondered how much it was worth. A second later, he felt like he was being watched. He took a look around, but saw no one.

"Delbert dear," Myrna called from the doorway of her room. "Will you toss the ball for Anthony while I take a shower?"

He shoved the bracelet back into his pocket.

Myrna came out holding Anthony and handed him to Del.

She headed back to her motel room, unaware someone had her in his visual scope.

Del pitched the ball towards the trees and Anthony retrieved it. "How long do I have to do this?" he muttered, and threw the ball harder.

He decided to contact a fence he knew. If he hocked the bracelet he could keep Al off his back.

After he'd finished his call, he looked up. No ball and no Anthony.

"Shit!" Del ran to the edge of the woods. "Anthony," he yelled.

Suddenly Myrna appeared behind him.

"Where's Anthony?" she demanded. "I thought you were watching him."

"Geez, you scared me." Del jumped, and ripped his pants on a bramble.

"Where's my pwescious baby?" She sounded hysterical.

"How the hell do I know?" He swatted a giant mosquito. "Maybe the little asshole took off after a cwazy wabbit."

"Are you making fun of me? I don't appreciate the foul language. How could you be so irresponsible?"

"Yeah, I know," he snapped." I'm dethspicable."

The ball came flying out of the woods as if someone had thrown it. Seconds later Anthony raced out into the open.

Myrna glared at Del, scooped up Anthony, and stomped off.

❖

Vern Haskins made his way back to his cabin, a shack he'd found empty twenty years ago, vacated by the hermit everyone had believed was the Hairy Man. He plopped down on his mattress and gazed at the worn photo of his deceased wife Helen.

He thought about the pretty woman he'd seen in the field earlier, the one with the dog. She looked like Helen. Then he thought about the oily guy he'd overheard on the cell phone. He was up to no good. It was something about money and killing, and he could read between the lines. Should he warn the woman? Would he be recognized? Was anyone even still searching for him?

He had made his home here after escaping from prison. He'd been framed for a murder he didn't commit. Framed by a man who had seduced Helen and then dumped her after conning her out of their life's savings. Ashamed and humiliated, Helen had threatened to turn him in to the police, so he'd strangled her. But the cops had pinned it on Vern.

He had forgiven Helen, but not her killer.

For years he'd kept the locals at bay by perpetuating the old Hairy Man legend, but he'd had a scare recently when a TV crew started snooping around.

"Helen," he said to the photo, "maybe it's time I rejoined the world." He'd never had the chance to avenge Helen's death, but at least he could keep another woman from harm. Maybe he'd just give the creep a good scare. He'd given the little doggie a bit of squirrel jerky when he had run into the woods after his ball. Maybe he could entice the dog to return, and get the man to follow.

❖

After registering Anthony for the next day's race, Myrna and Del strolled around Vergas a while without speaking.

"Sorry about this morning," Del finally said.

"I'm having second thoughts about this marriage, Del. I don't like being ridiculed, and I don't like my dog being put in danger. I thought I could trust you."

"You can! Give me another chance."

"We'll see."

❖

It was late afternoon when they returned to the motel.

"I'm tired," Myrna said.

"I'll take Anthony for a walk while you rest," Del offered.

"I don't know—"

"Please." He gave her his sad puppy dog look.

"All right, but make sure he stays on the leash."

"Yes, dear."

Del wondered if marrying her was such a good idea after all. Once they got back to Minneapolis, maybe he could just steal the rest of her jewelry and skip town.

He could have sworn he heard someone whistling in the woods. Anthony was pulling so hard on the leash that his collar slipped over his head and he dashed off into the trees.

"Stop!" Del screamed. He broke through the entangled branches and followed Anthony deep into the woods. He came to a clearing where Anthony was standing in front of a ramshackle cabin, wagging his tail and chewing on something.

"Come here," he yelled.

Out stepped a large dirty man with wild scraggly hair, wielding a hatchet. Terrified, Del turned to run, but tripped on a tree root. He looked up to see the Hairy Man standing directly over him.

Their eyes met and a look of horror came over both of their faces.

"Hello, Del. It's been awhile, hasn't it?" Vern said.

Del went pale.

"Vern? Is that you? Thank God. I thought you were—"

"The Hairy Man?" Vern said as he slammed the hatchet down.

"That was for Helen," he calmly said.

❖

Myrna was a wreck. Del and Anthony had been gone all night. Finally, at dawn, she called the sheriff.

"Do you think the Hairy Man got them?" she asked when he arrived.

He smiled. "Doubtful, ma'am. Why don't I check out the gentleman's room?"

When he returned, he held up a diamond bracelet. "This yours?"

"Why yes, it is."

"It was in your fiancé's room. I also noticed an illegal gambling site on his computer, so I made some calls. I hate to tell you this but there's a warrant out for his arrest. Delbert Gustafson is a known thief and con man, and he was a suspect in a murder investigation years ago. Maybe he just took off."

"He has my dog," Myrna sobbed.

"I'll let you know if we find him," the deputy said. "For now, just stay put."

❀

Vern looked into the cracked mirror on his cabin wall. He'd definitely aged, but after a bath, a haircut, and a shave, he cleaned up pretty good. He picked up Anthony, walked out of the woods, and knocked on Myrna's motel room door.

A red-eyed, disheveled Myrna opened the door.

"This your dog, Miss?"

"Pwescious!" she cried as Anthony leapt into her arms and licked her face.

"Where did you find him?"

"I have a cabin down the road," he lied. "Your dog must have gotten lost."

"Please, let me pay you."

"Absolutely not."

"If we hurry Anthony can still make the race. At least let me buy you dinner in town."

Vern hadn't had a restaurant meal in years. "Well, if you insist."

"I do," she said.

My name's Myrna, what's yours?" she asked.

Vern hesitated a moment. "It's Harold. Harold Mann."

Obsession

D. A. Lampi

Baudette, Minnesota, was a town where you could catch a hockey game nine months out of the year, and lutefisk was more common than tuna fish; a town where the winter blues were as ubiquitous as loon-size mosquitoes, and where everyone turned out for the county fair. The population was 1,106. Ariela, a thin twig of a woman as delicate as old porcelain, had hopes of making it 1,107.

Ariela had melancholic leanings and ramrod straight posture. A writer by trade, she covered the Baudette County Fair, the 4H Club, and peewee sports for the weekly *Baudette Times*. In her spare time, she decorated her nursery, more desperate each year as the peewee athletes became middle-school stars and her fertility plummeted. The baby had long since become her beautiful obsession, yet month after month, her dark, bitter, blood continued to flow.

At such times she found herself weeping at *Baby on Board* bumper stickers and fingering her trinkets. She took out her suitcase full of dinky Chinese finger traps, torn red tickets, and photos of the fair. It gave her sort of a grim pleasure to cuddle Keaton, the koala bear she'd won as a child, before packing away her dreams along with her trinkets for another month.

On their last morning together, Ariela woke with a tiny pinpoint of pain in her belly and a fertile boost of energy. It was already unbearably warm at seven a.m. Certain that she was ovulating, she reached for Nils. He flinched when she tried to draw him near, yelling that she was destroying their marriage. She covered her ears, muffling the sounds of her husband's anger. Nils refused to see it but, for Ariela, the certainty that there was a baby in her future dawned as bright as that summer morning and tempered her distress at the trial separation he'd recently proposed.

❂

"Baudette Realty," a voice answered.

Tearfully, she explained she needed a two-bedroom house with a yard and a short-term lease.

On the blistering hot day she moved, it was unimaginable that a Minnesota winter with air as bright and harsh as blades was a scant few months away. Nils helped take apart the crib and carry in the rocker. She pleaded with him to stay, but, with a peculiar intensity in his eyes that she found impossible to read, he carried the last box in and wished her well.

Late afternoon approached and shadows deepened. She assembled the nursery and decided to paint it pink. The smell of Mr. Clean gave the house a piney, homey smell but she couldn't rid herself of the feeling that there was something missing. She went downstairs, lit the gas stove and found a kettle, trying to put aside her longing. Children lived in such unsuitable homes, she mused, running her hands over her well-polished furniture. Her clean, well-kept house would be the perfect home to raise a child.

Exhausted from the move and the unpacking, she lit a cigarette with twitching fingers, dreaming of the warmth and happiness of her first Christmas in the new house. She hummed an odd, off-tune ditty as she wiped away cobwebs in the cabinets and put away her mother's teacups. While waiting for the tea to steep, Ariela inhaled the familiar nicotine-laced smoke and set the table with her mother's lace tablecloth and dainty teacups. Lemon-colored light faded as she and Keaton finished the last morsels of oatmeal cookies and sipped the last drops of sweetened tea.

Ariela washed the teacups and then, watching the clock, she opened and assembled the contents of the box she'd stored in the trunk of her car. A month ago, she'd watched a young family that should have been hers buy a stroller. She had gotten in her car and followed them to the trailer park. Weeks later, she'd gone into McCabe's for the same gray stroller. Mr. McCabe assured her it was the most popular model in town and then asked when she was due.

She practiced pushing it around the living room. After several attempts to fold it, she placed it in the trunk, her heart pounding in a way that frightened her, making her nauseous with fear. The time had come. It was the first day of the Baudette County fair. Nils would come back to her once he knew they had a child.

✻

She and Keaton drove slowly into town, holding onto happy memories of cotton candy and the day they'd first met. The fairgrounds loomed ahead. The wind carried the smell of popcorn and screams that rose and fell with each heart-stopping twist of the roller coaster. Almost time, she edged in next to a battered minivan and realized that its occupants—a mother, a father, two school-aged children, and a baby—were the same family she'd seen at McCabe's. It had to be a sign.

She stayed in her car and watched as the father took the stroller out of the minivan, opened it in one practiced move, and buckled the baby into the stroller. He locked the car with a resounding beep and called to the children—a boy and a girl—who skipped ahead. The mother lagged behind, and was, in Ariela's mind, distracted and inattentive.

Ariela took a hurried look around the parking lot before opening the trunk, unfolding the stroller and tucking a soft, yellow knitted blanket around Keaton. After pulling down the sunshade, she walked to the gate. So this was what it felt like to be a mother, she thought, aware of the sympathetic glances and the camaraderie of mothers. Soon, she herself would be a bona fide member of that glorious sisterhood.

A scowling carny with a cigarette between his lips stood at the gate. "That'll be six bucks."

"Per person?" If he had been born a dog, he would be a pit bull, she thought.

He peered into the stroller. "Yeah, per person. How old's the kid?"

"A baby," she muttered, taking out her wallet, her hand fluttering like a dust-colored moth. "One please."

He spit into the dust and glanced sideways at the stroller again before handing her a ticket. "Cute kid."

She looked at him in alarm, unsure whether he was joking. A crowd swam the length of the midway to the animal birthing center and she followed it, absorbed and excited by the prospect of birth. The stroller was light and easily maneuverable as she pushed it through the swarm of people heading for a wobbly-legged black and white calf nursing at its mother's distended udder.

The exhibit was standing room only. The dust and the smells of manure and cheap perfume made it difficult to breathe. For some inexplicable reason, Ariela felt saddened by the public display, and before leaving she looked deep into the cow's contented brown eyes, feeling a sort of sympathy with the animal. She tucked the yellow blanket tighter around Keaton and hurriedly left the building, pushing the stroller resolutely toward Madame Helga.

A neon sign flashed in the distance. Crystallomancy, Clairvoyance, Palmistry and Tasseography. Madame Helga stood in front of the small black tent. She was a toad-like woman dressed in colorful swirls of cotton skirts, which had the effect of making her appear even larger than she was. Her eyes were small and rheumy. Purplish curlicue veins ran the width of her nose and cheeks. Her wracking cough had a life of its own. She peered at Ariela through pince-nez glasses and led her through a heavy black velvet drape into a smaller room.

Madame Helga's flowered skirt rose as she sat at a cloth-covered card table, revealing white, fish gut-colored legs with bulging ropey veins. Her feet were dirty and stuffed into sandals like fat sausages. Long, black hair shone with grease and hung limply down her broad back.

Her hands were cold as she took Ariela's hands into her own and looked at her palms. Her fingernails held a purplish tint. "Hmmmm … Hmmmm … I can vaguely make something out here … I can almost see it."

"Is it a girl or a boy?" Ariela asked. The tent's thick black curtains wavered, closing in on her, exciting and terrifying at the same time.

"The image is fading," the fortuneteller said, glancing at the stroller. "But I believe it's a boy."

Ariela gasped. She had a girl's name picked out—Giovanna—a gift from God. Every image she'd had of herself as a mother had been as a mother of a girl. An eerie silence filled the darkened tent. "Are you sure?" she whispered.

The fortuneteller's face lit up. "For an additional ten dollars I can read the tea leaves. The leaves near the rim will tell us what is going to happen in the very near future."

Ariela drank the bitter brew, held the nearly empty teacup in her left hand, gave it three swirls, and gently dumped the remaining liquid into a saucer according to Madame Helga's instructions. "What is it? What do you see?" She held her breath as the murky green leaves clung to the sides of the cup. *Breathe. Just breathe, she told herself.*

Madame Helga peered into the teacup and paled. "I see a man in white. Many unknowns. A hospital perhaps."

"But is it a boy or a girl?"

Her porcine eyes darting to the entrance of the tent, Madame Helga whispered hoarsely, "A boy. I'm sorry. That's all I can tell you."

Ariela's breath came in quick, loud gasps. She stumbled into a dark and moonless night with a midway lit up like Christmas Eve, humming a ragged tune as she wandered the fairgrounds, pushing the gray stroller.

❀

They stood in line for the Ferris wheel. The children held paper cones of cotton candy and jumped with excitement, their mouths stained the color of blueberries, while the father bought their tickets. Ariela stood in the shadows and watched as the father and his children climbed into the gondola-like car. The night grew quiet. Tiny sparkling lights illuminated the Ferris wheel's spokes and lit up the sky.

She waited, mesmerized by what looked like the lights of a thousand stars. The children waved each time the giant wheel made another rotation. She inched closer and parked her stroller next to the baby. A blue blanket—just as Madame Helga had predicted! He sucked on a pacifier, his cheeks puffing in and out, fat and pink. The mother laughed and snapped pictures of her husband and children. Just one more rotation.

When the children were at the wheel's highest point, and the mother craned her neck to see them, Ariela took a quick breath and stepped toward the baby's stroller. Afterwards, with Keaton left behind, she slipped into the midway as soundlessly as a gator into a dark pond.

❀

Ariela pushed the stroller to the gate, plucked the baby out of it and into the car seat, and loaded the gray stroller into the car with the practiced moves of an experienced mother. The baby opened his eyes and gave a small cry as she started the car. "There, there," she clucked. "We'll get you to bed as soon as we get home."

In the two-bedroom house, his fat cheeks worked double time as he sucked at the bottle. He had perfect pudgy hands with nails as delicate as an amphibian's third eyelid. She rocked him, basking in the glory of motherhood, and then closed her eyes and bent down to smell his new-baby smell. He cooed and the music began to swell. Her breasts tingled.

He was a symphony of sights and sounds and smells, elevating her to unfathomable heights and taking her places she'd never been. She'd call him Gabriel, her angel.

She changed his diaper and dressed him in pink pajamas, promising him they'd soon go shopping and outfit him in blue. He'd have the best of everything—a real house, a real mother. As she held him in the rocker, dreaming of what she would give him, searchlights beaming through the windows suddenly illuminated the room. She covered his eyes, wrapped Gabriel as tight as a pig-in-a-blanket and stood behind the drapes.

From behind the nylon curtains, she made out a gray sedan in the drive. The driver killed the engine, got out of the car and walked to the door. He was a tall man, dressed in dark-colored clothes; she knew him well. A loud knock at the door shattered the silence. Ariela huddled behind the drapes and held the baby close. Gabriel opened his eyes and smiled a toothless happy grin. A wondrous, blissful kind of love blossomed in that smile.

"Ariela. Open the door. It's me. Nils."

Gabriel stirred in her arms. "Shh, it's okay," she murmured, adjusting the bottle. "Go back to sleep."

The knocking grew louder. Sirens howled in the distance. "Ariela. Open the door. I know about the baby. We can talk about this," Nils said in a voice loud enough to startle the baby. The sound of sirens shrieking came closer. She grew frightened, and then angry—she and Gabriel were bonding. This was *their* special time. She'd waited so long for this moment.

Within minutes, flashing lights were everywhere. Squad cars, the volunteer fire department, news vans—all of them were shining their god-awful lights into the house. Gabriel opened his eyes and gave a high-pitched cry. "It's okay," she said, becoming flustered. "There's nothing to worry about. Mama's here." She crossed the living room to look outside the back window. The tall oaks moved like malevolent sentinels stealthily toward the house. She gripped the baby tighter.

The oaks continued moving toward her house. Trembling, she laid the baby in the stroller, covered him with the yellow blanket, and pushed him away from the window. Frantically, she considered her options, taking a hesitant step toward the kitchen. Nils knocked again, shaking the house with the force of his knock. A cold, disembodied voice filled the air. "Come to the door where we can see you. Keep your hands up. There's nothing to worry about."

She looked at the baby, asleep in the stroller. Her breath came out in spurts as she pushed open the kitchen door and opened the cabinet. The shelves were newly papered and everything had its place. Her mother's flowered teacups were stacked two deep. She reached behind them, felt the smooth metal.

The cold, hard weight of it in her hand reassured her. She gripped the pistol firmly. With the webbing between her index finger and her thumb flush on the grip, she reached for the trigger guard. Her Gabriel was still asleep, his thumb in his sweet mouth.

"Ariela, open the door," Nils called with that edge she'd always hated in his voice. "They know you're there. What in the world do you think you're doing taking a baby from his mother?"

She walked to the front door and stood there for a moment, listening. She was his mother. She had sworn to protect him. The oaks were still there—they were coming toward her to take him away. Was Nils in collusion with them? Had he ever really wanted the baby?

Gabriel let out a shrill cry from the living room. She opened the door, gun in hand, and said, "I am his mother. Me. They don't deserve him. I do. You'll never take him from me." And then she aimed and fired.

Carpe Diem or
Murder at the Carp Fest

M. E. Bakos

"Carp Fest. It's a silly name for a festival," I protested to my new neighbor, the charming Patrick O'Neil. Patrick had recently moved into our little neighborhood which bordered the Coon Rapids Dam. He had a shock of white hair and a lean athletic build.

"My dear Becca, it's a glorious day. Anoka has their Halloween Capitol, Hopkins has their raspberries." He threw open his arms enthusiastically. "Coon Rapids has their carp. *Carpe diem!* That's what the festival founders undoubtedly wanted."

"Ah, seize the day," I said wryly. "You have a bit of trivia for every occasion."

"It's my thing. The phrase is Latin, you know." Patrick grinned widely and his blue eyes twinkled behind steel-rimmed glasses.

We had decided to spend the first weekend of June enjoying the local color of the two-day festival that featured food vendors, music, and DNR nature tents. The crowning touch was a fishing contest where the winner became the proud owner of a "carp-mobile" and fishing boat. The carp-mobile was a minivan donated by a local dealer and decorated with an animated picture of a carp.

It was the first day of the event. From our walks together, I'd learned Patrick was widowed, as I was. My house faced the street with the walking and biking path that led to the dam. He lived a street over, in a house on a cul-de-sac. We had struck up a friendship based on our mutual availability for daily walks. He had an affinity for trivia and chattered on while we walked. I was given more to taking in the scenery and appreciated the companionship.

"Okay, what kind of fish is a carp? Besides being a homely one."

Patrick cleared his throat, and spoke in a voice he had likely used in his thirty-five years as a history and science teacher, "The word 'carp' refers to a group of freshwater fish."

As Patrick started to go into unbearable detail about carp, I spotted Roxanne Randall, my nemesis from my old job. She was stuffing cotton candy down her throat in front of a vendor that was parked on the grassy lawn of the dam's park.

I gasped and quickly ducked behind a tree.

Even from a distance, I could see her greedy green eyes magnified by the thick lenses of her eyeglasses as she ogled the vendor's wares. Unusual, I thought. The vain Roxanne usually wore her glasses perched atop her head. And often forgot they were there.

"And they are edible." Patrick stopped talking and looked bewildered at my abrupt departure. "Becca? Is something the matter?"

I stood stalk still behind the huge trunk of a cottonwood and hissed. "It's that witch from A & D Shoes—the one that tried to get me fired."

"Becca, it seems to me very unlikely that any employer would deem you unemployable." Patrick's voice was soothing.

"You don't know the power of that woman Roxanne. She wormed her way into every facet of the business and before I knew it, the owners, managers, and customers were all trilling what a gem Roxanne Randall was.

"She got more and more floor time, and I was stuck in the stockroom organizing the shoe boxes. She's the reason I jumped ship to A & E Shoe Company—A & D's biggest competitor." I nearly spit remembering the antics Roxanne Randall had used to get ahead in the footwear industry.

My eyes narrowed as I watched Roxanne's substantial bulk move from the cotton candy vendor to a hot dog vendor. She'd always had a problem with food. Seeing her stuff herself gave me a small feeling of satisfaction. Until I thought of the final day she had maneuvered me off floor sales to stockroom duties. The memory still rankled.

It had happened a day before the long Memorial holiday weekend. I was scheduled for four days off—rare in retail sales. People bought shoes 24/7, and A & D Shoes was the top store in the region.

My best customer, Bernice Preston, spent thousands of dollars on shoes at a time, so I'd cater to her every whim. She'd make appointments with me to see the new collections, and then buy several pairs in different colors. That time, Roxanne had taken Bernice's call and assured Bernice I would be available for her. Of course, she knew I'd be on vacation.

When Bernice went in to look at the shoes I'd ordered for her approval, Roxanne had rung in all my carefully prepared cards under her own sales code. She'd taken credit for my sales, and neither Bernice, nor the store owners were any the wiser.

When I'd gotten back from vacation, my manager took me to the back room and reassigned my duties as stock room coordinator. I remembered the grim look on the shoe repairman Ed's face as I was led past his counter.

I'd immediately given notice, and jumped ship to A & E Shoes. Little did I know A & D's fortunes were tanking; within six months they were bankrupt.

After the company's collapse, I learned the manager that had demoted me was an uncle of the despicable Roxanne. He'd been newly hired to "right size" the failing business and was on a mission to promote Roxanne and get rid of anyone in her way.

"What on earth is Roxanne Randall doing at the Carp Fest?" I asked Patrick. Roxanne didn't seem like someone who would be seen at a local festival.

"Not enough prestige?" Patrick said.

Then it hit me. I remembered Roxanne's husband was a big time fisherman. She had bragged loudly to anyone about her *personal nurse* (he was an RN) husband Jeffrey. Then she would smile and explain how he had once again caught the biggest walleye at the fishing opener. Or whatever other contest he was in. That must be it—I didn't think she lived in the area.

I shivered at the thought of Roxanne's antics casting gloom on a splendidly sunlit day at the dam.

"Becca, don't let her bother you," Patrick chuckled. "After all, you came out far better on the job front than she did."

"I did. I did indeed." After working at A & E Shoes for a while, I'd left and opened my own shoe salon, selling to wealthy residents of Wayzata and Minnetonka. Bernice had followed me and referred all her well-off friends to my new salon. I had done well. When I'd later sold the business, I retained a controlling interest that provided a nice income for an early retirement.

Yet, seeing Roxanne brought back all the horrors of my time at A & D Shoes.

I hung back, keeping my distance from Roxanne as Patrick and I visited the different displays, but my eyes wandered periodically to check on her and her immense appetite—an appetite currently being fed by a pizza vendor.

"What's going on?" Patrick's voice rose to a high tenor as we walked. A crowd had gathered just beyond the pizza booth. I followed his gaze, and gulped when I saw a bulky body laid flat out on the sidewalk.

"It's Roxanne!"

"Really, Becca, how could you know that from this distance?" Patrick asked.

"I'd know that shoe anywhere!" Earlier, I'd caught a glimpse of the high-end walking shoes that Roxanne was wearing. They were imported, designed for comfort, not so much for modest budgets. If I hadn't worked in the business, I'd have balked at the hundreds of dollars they cost.

We approached the gathering crowd.

"She's dead," a Park Patrol officer said. He was on his knees, bent over Roxanne's body. I maneuvered between a woman with a stroller and the back of a muscle-bound, six-foot-tall man to get a better look.

Roxanne was on her back. The partially eaten slice of pepperoni pizza had dropped and left a grease spot at her side. Her sleeveless top displayed bare shoulders. A tiny drop of what looked like blood dotted her left bicep. Her head had twisted to the side in the fall and curly red hair covered the side of her face. Her glasses were pushed at an odd angle, her stare vacant in death.

I backed out of the crowd when I was satisfied it was Roxanne, and turned back to Patrick. "Well, ding dong."

"A bit harsh, don't you think, Becca?" Patrick gently rebuked me.

"Oh, I suppose. She was just such a terror." I shuddered at the memory of Roxanne grilling me like a sergeant about something as trivial as a price tag. "The prices *must* be written in *red*," she'd screamed at me. It was ironic when everyone knew she could barely see the tags without her glasses. Flabbergasted, I'd walked away. The store was always empty when she had those temper tantrums. She was a master of turning on the charm when a customer or a manager was within earshot.

An ambulance and fire truck, alarms blaring, quickly reached the scene. Some of the new arrivals attended to Roxanne's body while others directed the crowd to move along.

Patrick and I left along with the other curiosity-seekers. "What do you suppose happened?" he asked. We were on the river path back to our respective homes. The promise of the day's activities had dimmed with Roxanne's death.

She was probably murdered, I thought. But I said, "I guess it was a heart attack. The woman always had a problem with food. Who eats cotton candy and pepperoni pizza at her age?"

"Well, maybe one or the other, but probably not both," Patrick said.

"Certainly not all at the same time," I said.

We had reached the street where we usually parted to take our separate routes home. "Well, Becca, shall we do it again tomorrow? It couldn't be any worse than today's events." Patrick reached over and patted my arm.

I shrugged as I left the street and headed towards my house. "Sure. A good band will be playing anyway." The festival wrapped up its activities with local musicians and the announcement of the winner of the carp-mobile.

"Same time, okay?" he said.

"Works for me." I nodded then let myself into my house.

I puttered around the house the rest of the day, musing over Roxanne Randall's death. I'm not a vengeful person, but someone else might be, I reasoned, if Roxanne had continued to pull the same stunts at A & D Shoes after I'd left. She might have had an enemy or two out there. I pondered the matter while I potted new baskets for the deck.

What if it *was* murder?

After the shoe company went bankrupt, it had been bought out by another company called Shoe World. Many of the same people who worked there had been with A & D.

I decided to pay them a visit.

❁

There was something about a shoe store that still warmed my blood: the smells, the styles, the colors. Ask any shoe devotee, and they'll tell you the same thing. I'd spent a number of years shopping the competition for my own shoe stores. But I was there looking for someone who might have had a grudge against Roxanne.

I paused at the repair counter to see Ed, the shoe repair and dye expert from A & D Shoes, who now worked for Shoe World. "Ed, how have you been?"

"Well, well, Rebecca Hartwood. Good to see you," the short, balding man behind the counter exclaimed. "Say, did you hear about Roxanne Randall?" He stopped hammering a new heel on a shoe.

"I did. I was at the park when it happened, and saw her body. I even noticed her footwear. She was wearing that funny looking imported walking shoe."

"Did you see the color?"

"They were red. It was Roxanne's favorite color as I recall."

"An orange red." He pushed up his glasses. "She dyed them herself. She mixed the color here, and took the bottle home to dye the shoes. I couldn't be trusted to do the job," he grumbled. "Thirty years in the business, and she had to do her own dye job."

"That was Roxanne. Controlling to the end."

Ed barked a short laugh and nodded. "Yeah. That was Roxanne Randall, all right."

A customer came up to the counter and asked about stretching a pair of shoes from a six to a seven. Ed sighed as he told the woman, "No it can't be done."

I winked and nodded goodbye as I overheard the woman say, "But they are such a good deal."

I lingered over the displays of footwear, drinking in the sight of sassy high heels, low heeled walking shoes, and the season's new sandals. I left with a sense of longing for a new pair.

❀

Patrick arrived promptly the next morning for the second day of the Carp Fest. His eyes were twinkling. "Are you ready for the day's activities, Becca?"

"As ready as ever."

Rock and roll music greeted us as we strode down the path. We slowed our pace as we reached the dam. I was distracted by the crowd of people congregating at the booth where the winners of the fishing contest were announced. A large man was making the announcements. "Jeffrey Randall wins this year's carp-mobile with the biggest carp caught in the contest. Congratulations Jeffrey!" The crowd politely clapped, while others drifted away.

"Huh. Randall?" I stood with Patrick, squinting at the man on the stage. "Could that be Roxanne's husband?" I was puzzled.

A woman turned to me. "Yes, it is," she said slyly as she moved away from the group.

"*The woman who died here yesterday?*" I asked.

The woman gave one last nod and left.

"Unbelievable!" As much as I disliked Roxanne, it seemed remarkable her husband would be here the day after her death to claim a win.

"They probably had issues," Patrick said.

"Issues, *indeed*," I sputtered.

I looked to where Jeffrey Randall had gone. He stood grinning amid the crowd with the keys to the prized carp-mobile dangling in his hand. Then I noticed that several uniformed officers were approaching him through the crowd. Suddenly one of the officers surprised him and deftly secured his wrists in handcuffs behind his back.

His grins turned to angry scowls. "I didn't do it. I tell you I didn't do it!" he yelled as he was led away to the back of a police car. He looked greasy and unshaven, and his shirt was stained and wrinkled.

"Well, there you go. Roxanne's death must have looked suspicious. The spouse is always the first suspect. The police probably set the whole thing up so that he wouldn't disappear. He'd be sure to claim his prize," Patrick said.

It looked like there was going to be another broadcast. The same announcer called, "There's been a change in the winner. The carp-mobile actually goes to John Kaminski." He motioned to a young man standing beside him. "Give the man a hand for landing the biggest fish this weekend!"

The crowd gave a smattering of applause, then went back to talking about the shocking arrest.

"I'm not so sure about Jeffrey. How could he have killed her? He was on a fishing boat when she collapsed," I said.

We started to take the river path back to our homes.

"That, my dear Becca, is a police matter." Patrick leaned over and gave me a peck on the cheek. "Shall we walk again tomorrow morning? *Carpe diem?*" he called out as I opened my screen door.

"Yes. *Carpe diem,*" I agreed.

I spent the rest of the day absorbed with Jeffrey Randall's arrest, and what I'd observed about Roxanne's body. When I couldn't let it go, I made a couple of phone calls. Then I went to Shoe World.

❖

Ed was in his usual location, explaining to a woman that he couldn't resole her favorite athletic shoes. "It's not a material that will take a new sole, ma'am," he replied patiently to the woman who sighed, took her shoes, and walked away.

"Hi, Ed."

"Rebecca, you're back awfully soon. You heard Roxanne's husband was arrested for her murder?"

"Yes. In fact, I was there when it happened." I looked squarely at him. "Ed, Why did you do it?"

"I don't know what you're talking about," he said, looking at his work table.

"You killed Roxanne. You knew it was only a matter of time before she used the spare bottle of insulin she kept at work. You had laced it with shoe dye."

"She took the dye home."

"You kept just enough dye to spike her insulin. I noticed a slightly different shade of red at her injection site. Instead of a pinkish red, it was more of an orange red."

Ed's face turned a deep purple. "You knew what she was like. She was hell bent on closing my department. I was going to be out of a job after thirty years. Thirty years of shoe repair! She'd say in that mocking tone of hers, that 'people don't fix shoes, they buy new.'"

He snatched up a hammer and lunged. I ducked. He missed. Frantically, I moved to get out of the door. He lunged again, hurling the hammer like a spear, narrowly missing my head.

"STOP," I yelled, and turned to face him.

He picked up another hammer and held it high above his head, his face contorted as he rounded the counter.

Then two officers came out from behind the side door, and one yelled, "Drop it!"

Patrick had waited outside with the officers. He took my hand and we watched as the officers cuffed Ed and led him away.

"I'm curious, Becca. What made you think it was Ed and not Jeffrey that murdered Roxanne?" Patrick asked.

"It was the color of the drop at what I figured was the injection site on Roxanne's arm. At first I thought it was blood, but that didn't sit right with me. I know people use colored insulin so they can see where the injection is. The dot matched the color of Roxanne's shoes. Jeffrey would know the lack of insulin could cause coma, but not necessarily death. Ed knew that toluene, the toxic chemical in shoe dye, was lethal. Roxanne was dead on the spot."

"Quite right, Becca."

"And with her eyesight, she probably couldn't tell the bottle had been tampered with."

"Ghastly business, Becca."

"Good grief," I added.

"So, another walk tomorrow morning?" Patrick asked.

"Yes, of course. Seize the day!"

Iced

Susan Koefod

Henry Shaw blew into town every January with the bitter north wind. The moment he arrived, we knew it was over for the rest of us, even though his winning Winter Carnival ice sculpture entry never varied from year to year. His was the Mona Lisa to our best efforts: our glistening birds, shimmering creatures, and fantastical machines simply could not compete with his genius-level work. No one knew better the agony of losing to him than me: I finished second every year to Henry Shaw.

I might have had a chance of winning the year he wound up dead—his skull split by his own chisel and his beautiful ice sculpture dashed to bits—except that I was instantly considered the prime suspect in his murder.

Of course I resented his genius. I'm no angel. His death would surely have cleared the way for me to win the contest at last. But of all the competitors, I was the closest Shaw had to a friend. In the final hours before his death, I learned what haunted him to sculpt the same woman, again and again. I alone knew the true identity of his killer, but feared that what I saw the night he was killed would do little to convince the authorities of my innocence.

❀

Shaw achieved his artistry using worn, old-fashioned carving tools, leaving us to wonder what he might have gained by the advanced technology available—laser-guided chain saws, 3D computer models—not that any of us wanted to point out the merits of upgrading to him. He wasn't slowed at all by his humble gear. He chipped and shaped the thick block of ice rapidly, working with a steady urgency, as if he were a heart surgeon trying to save a dying patient. He talked to no one, and worked around the clock.

I always made a special effort, every year, to be friendly with Shaw. I felt it my duty to show good sportsmanship to the other carvers and Shaw himself. But Shaw seemed deaf to my courteous greetings.

"Why do you even bother?" Jess Laux, an up-and-coming young French-Canadian sculptor said to me the day before Shaw was killed. I was, as usual, buying two cups of coffee and a couple of toasted bagels from a food truck vendor.

"What are you hoping to gain by brown-nosing the guy? Trying to exploit a weak spot? Learn his secrets?"

"Just trying to be a good sport," I said, tossing a couple of sugar and creamer packets in my pockets before balancing a bagel on each of the coffee cups' plastic lids.

"I wish the guy would disappear," Jess said. "I'm tired of him winning every year. Aren't you about ready to kill him?"

"Now, now ..." I said to the young guy. "Never let competition affect your actions or character."

He muttered a French-Canadian epithet and stomped away. With that, I picked up the cups—noticing that the coffee was so hot the cups warmed my hands through my thick buckskin choppers.

I carried breakfast to Shaw, and as usual he seemed only vaguely aware that I had dropped by. His look was distant, his mind clearly on the work he was sculpting.

I couldn't help but whistle in appreciation of the beauty that was emerging from the ice. I knew, having closely observed Shaw in the past, that it was the same woman once again. Yet she was even more beautiful than she had been the year before. Her serene face held a wide-set pair of ice-blue eyes. Her long, wavy hair flew in frozen whorls around her face, tousled by an unearthly breeze. She wore an almost transparent gown of silky ice, of a vintage style that made her appear timeless yet part of the distant past.

She was frozen in time and ice.

That year she seemed more real than ever—if such a thing was possible—as if the right combination of wishes and alchemy might bring her to life. I wondered again if there was a real woman who looked just like the ice sculpture.

"Who is she?" I said to Shaw. Shaw said nothing, even though he glanced distractedly in my direction, as if he'd awoken from a nightmare. His eyes darted around, then seemed to fix on something in the distance.

A painful look appeared in his bloodshot eyes.

I followed his line of sight to see what had transfixed him so and saw a woman in a heavy hooded cloak watching him sculpt from not far off. A sudden gust of wind blew her hood off, exposing her long wavy hair.

It was her! The very woman Shaw had been carving all of these years. She was just as beautiful as her frozen image. I glanced at the ice sculpture, confirming that indeed it was the very same woman. When I turned to look at the real woman again, she had vanished.

Shaw's shoulders slumped in disappointment, and he turned back to the sculpture.

"It was her!" I shouted at him, my hands shaking from excitement. I dribbled the hot coffee and scorched the exposed skin between my heavy gloves and my jacket wristbands. I bobbled both bagels onto the snow.

Shaw dismissed me with a shrug, and went straight back to his carving.

"Who is she?" I demanded, my wrists blistering. "Why aren't you going after her?"

Shaw didn't budge. I couldn't believe that he seemed uninterested in seeking out the real woman who inspired and haunted him.

I set off to find her, and thought I saw her in the distance, making her way along the riverfront boulevard. She hurried along the sidewalk that edged the top of the river bluff, not noticing the steep drop-off just a few footsteps away and the icy and impassable Mississippi below. Another gust of wind sent her cloak flapping, her hair flying. Before I could catch up to her, she disappeared into a crowd gathered around the dreaded Winter Carnival Vulcans, their faces smudged with soot. These kings of fire symbolized the coming warmer season. Ultimately they would defeat winter, symbolized by King Boreas and his Royal Court, at the end of the carnival.

The mysterious woman had the regal bearing and classic beauty of royalty, and her cloak was of the style of the long capes worn by the king and his entourage, but her otherworldly appearance, so much like her frozen doppelganger, made it seem like she was from another realm.

My heart began to slow, and as it did, I realized that the wild chase I'd gone on was ridiculous. I looked around to see if Laux had noticed my bizarre behavior, but he was nowhere near.

I had been taken in by Shaw's obsession, as if standing so near to him and watching his masterpiece emerge, year after year, had somehow infected me with the same mania. Or perhaps it was a simple matter of the long, hard work of sculpting and the heated competition that was getting to me. I shook it off. I had my own sculpture to finish, and needed every minute I had left to get it done.

I laughed at my foolishness. When I walked back to my ice slab, I passed by Shaw and saw him working at his usual pace. He was so absorbed he didn't see me. But I couldn't help but take one last look in the direction where the scarlet-clad Vulcan Crewe devilishly taunted the spectators around them. The mysterious woman was nowhere to be seen.

❁

I worked nonstop for the rest of the day and late into the evening. It was the last day of the contest and judging would occur early the next morning. Though I could think of a dozen more touches I would have liked to make on my sculpture, I was bone tired, and growing colder by the minute. The temperature plunged into the single digits with wind chills—from the cutting wind—dipping below zero. Except for Shaw, I was the only other sculptor still working on an entry. It was eerily quiet, except for the quiet chipping of Shaw's tools, as all the other sculptors' power tools were shut off. Though I had some battery-powered lights to help illuminate my work area, Shaw worked under the available street-lights, which made it difficult to do all of the fine detailing required at this stage, though that never seemed to be a problem for him.

I yawned and shivered, and decided to go rest and warm up in my truck for an hour or two, then return refreshed to make the last few changes to my piece. The rules allowed the sculptors to work right up to the judging hour, all night long if someone chose, and typically it was the two of us—Shaw and me—who worked through that last night.

I fell asleep quickly in my truck, exhausted by the long hours of work and the strange escapade with Shaw's model. I set the alarm on my cell phone to awaken me at three a.m., but was startled awake by a loud crash outside. Fearing that some weak spot in my ice sculpture had given way, I hurriedly rubbed the frost off my truck window and looked out to see what had happened.

But there was nothing wrong with my piece. I then peered through the opening in the frost in Shaw's direction, squinting to see his sculpture in the dim light of the streetlights. I could see what I thought was his sculpture, but then swore I saw it moving. Without a thought, I opened my door and hurried over.

When I heard his sculpture speak, I stopped in my tracks. An agonizing sound came from her throat, a raw pain thawing to tenderness, like frost-bitten limbs warming to life.

She moved, her glassy gown crackling around her, and, in a moment, she was transformed into the same mysterious woman I had seen earlier that day. Yet she was also the same woman he had been carving, over and over for so many years. They had become one and the same. But had the real woman merged with and animated the statue, or had the ice come alive under the artist's hands to produce a newborn, fully formed woman?

I saw something flashing in her hand. It was one of Shaw's chisels. Shaw backed away from her, and in doing so tripped over the shards of ice that he had chipped away while sculpting. He fell to the ground heavily and she dropped to his side.

I crept closer, hypnotized by the beautiful woman bent over the prone sculptor. I swore I heard her say "Darling," to him. And "My love."

And then, "Be with me forever." Then she held the chisel over his forehead and came down on him hard.

I screamed, and she saw me. She dropped the chisel, rose to her feet, and disappeared into the midnight shadows of the winter-stripped trees of Kellogg Park.

Shaw lay dead beneath the wreckage of his sculpture.

❁

Even though I had immediately called 911 to alert the police to Shaw's death and tell them the main suspect had gotten away, I was slapped in handcuffs and hauled off.

They questioned me all day long and far into the evening. When I told them about the woman I saw, how she was an exact twin of the sculptures Shaw had carved every year, they laughed.

I repeated my story, never wavering from it, yet never seeming to convince them of its truth.

There were two detectives interviewing me, and they stepped aside to have a brief conversation. The older guy, a slouchy, stained fellow with thinning hair, sent the younger detective out of the room. When he came back twenty minutes later, he showed his boss a photo he'd apparently printed off the web. The old guy nodded and set the picture on the table in front of me.

"That's her," I said, jabbing my finger at the photo. "Who is she? Why aren't you looking for her?" It was a high quality black and white photo, a professional shot. The woman leaned against a blank wall, her head back, her wavy hair cascading around her shoulders, her adoring eyes on the photographer. I knew in a moment that the photographer must be Shaw. Only a man who had experienced that look in her eyes— the look of complete devotion—would be able to render it in sculpture. She was wearing the simple gown Shaw had expertly captured in ice.

When I asked again for the identity of the woman in the photo, the investigators looked at each other—the looks on their faces suggesting I might be insane. Or the worst liar they'd ever encountered.

"Well?" I said. "Tell me who she is."

"It's Henry Shaw's wife," the lead investigator said.

"His wife?"

"You heard that right," he said.

"So have you found her yet?" I said. "Brought her in for questioning?" The older guy looked like he was about to laugh.

The younger detective answered. "That's not going to happen."

"And why not?" I demanded.

"She's been dead for twenty years."

❈

Her framed photo sits on a small table in my room, where the light is best. I can see it from almost every angle of my tiny room—it's the first thing I see when I wake in the morning, the last thing I see before falling asleep at night.

I see her in my dreams.

I've been told it would be better for my sanity if the photo weren't displayed so prominently, as if it were a religious icon I worshipped. But the one time it was taken away from me, I fell into a deep depression, and was moments from committing suicide when the guards stopped me.

I was convicted of killing Henry Shaw: my fingerprints were on the murder weapon. I had picked it up in those initial moments of confusion when I discovered Shaw dead, and saw the icy phantom of his deceased wife slipping away. I had hurried out of my truck so quickly that I neglected to put on my buckskin choppers.

Beyond the evidence of my fingerprints on the murder weapon, there were enough character witnesses—including Jess Laux—to convince the jury that I was guilty. Laux's testimony was the most damning; he'd said that I'd sworn to kill Shaw in order to win the contest. In fact, it was Laux who'd come up with the idea of killing Shaw, not me. But my lawyer would not let me take the stand to rebut Laux or any of the other witnesses' testimony. And once I'd been convicted, my lawyer said the best we could hope for was for me to be committed to an asylum.

He got his wish.

As the years go by, I understand Shaw better and better. Sometimes I think I have become him. I've often sketched her image, from memory, and when I do, I think of Shaw sculpting her in ice from memory. When death released him from his obsession, that same obsession was born anew in me. Its grip has been as tenacious as a never-ending winter.

Late at night I am often awakened from my sleep by what sounds like the north wind rushing through the drafty asylum corridors. And then I swear I see her, floating by in her translucent dress, her face glowing under the safety lights, her wavy tresses stirring lightly as she turns to me.

Bobcat Days Medallion Hunt

Christine Husom

D amon "Digger" Borden pulled the office blind back far enough to
see the gathering crowd, but not enough to be noticed. He spotted
James Von Eck, and a sense of anticipation—bordering on excitement—
mixed in with the blood coursing through his body and speeded its flow.
He'd waited years for the right time to carry out his plan, and that time
had finally arrived.

He glanced at his watch: 8:42 a.m. The twenty-fourth annual Bobcat Days Medallion Hunt would begin in eighteen minutes. There were
already between fifty and sixty people of all ages forming casual lines,
waiting to pick up the first clue. And with good reason. The first one
to find the medallion would win a sweet one thousand dollars in prize
money. Not bad for a half day's work.

Borden geared himself up, ready to perform his official duties as
mayor—welcoming everyone to the kick-off event of the annual Bobcat
Days Festival and handing out the first clue to each of the folks. There
was a special clue he'd personally written for James Von Eck. One that
Borden would unofficially deal from the bottom of the stack so James
could begin a medallion hunt customized just for him.

"Hey Digger. Sorry, I guess I should call you Mayor, huh?" It was
Suzy, a former classmate who was visiting from out of town.

He extended his hand and gave her his best smile, practiced over
and over until it looked genuine. "Good to see you, Suzy, and you call me
whatever you'd like. Within reason, of course." He gave a little chuckle.
"You're looking great, by the way."

"Thanks, Digger, and you too. Hey, I've heard rumors they're starting
to plan our fifteen-year class reunion next summer. Can you believe we
graduated fourteen years ago already?"

"Hard to believe, all right."

"And we're lucky, compared to the class before us. We've only lost two classmates. Mindy had that sudden heart attack last year, which I still cannot believe! And Will. That was the worst, to disappear like that. They never did figure out what happened to him."

"No, they never did." *And they never will.* "Well, I'd better take my official position."

"Catch ya later."

Digger. "Little Digger" was the nickname his father had given him when he was a small boy, and eventually "little" was dropped when he got older. He'd liked tagging along when his father got a call to dig a grave. Mostly he watched from the sidelines, but once in a while he got to sit next to his father on the backhoe.

Digger had taken over the business when his father left town, and continued to run it as a second job after he'd gotten elected mayor. It was far more lucrative than what he earned as the top official of small town Bobcat, Minnesota. Besides, he'd run for office for one reason alone, and it wasn't the money.

Digger had gotten the call from Pete at the funeral home three days before, requesting a grave be dug for a 4:00 p.m. Saturday burial. The timing was perfect and Digger set his plan in motion. The folks in Bobcat would be occupied searching for the valuable medallion, unaware there was another event going on at the Memorial Gardens Cemetery.

Promptly at nine o'clock, Mayor Borden raised his hands above his head. "Can I have everybody's attention please?" The voices from the crowd quieted down. "Welcome to the kick-off event of our week-long festival. And what a day. The temperature is supposed to stay in the eighties with no humidity to speak of. That should help keep the mosquitos to a minimum.

"Okay. We'll go over the three rules. One: no one starts until everyone has the first clue. Two: everyone over age twelve works on the clues all by themselves." Digger waved his hand in a shooing motion. "Kids under twelve, you go ahead and help your parents. Three: leave the clues at each spot for the next guy. Okay then, let's get this show on the road."

Mayor Borden did his best to appear as cool as a cucumber, but when he noticed James Von Eck moving closer, five or six people back, beads of sweat popped from his glands. "Getting warm in the sun," he remarked to no one in particular.

"Digger." James smiled and held out his hand.

"James. Good luck, buddy." *Ha,* he thought as he deftly pulled the clue from the bottom of the stack. Digger knew James' wife Joni was working that day. The stir would come in the evening when James hadn't returned home and Joni would have no idea where he was. Digger alone would know the answer to that, and it was a secret he would take to his own grave.

It seemed like half a lifetime until Digger handed out the final clue and announced, "May the best person win."

❂

James moved to the side of the crowd and studied the first clue. "A double width hangout from years gone by, where more than one kiss was shared under the sky." *Double width. That's one way to describe Wide Street where kids gathered night after night, figuring out where to go and what to do.* The first clue was always the easiest.

He jogged to Wide Street and spent a minute locating the spot described as "where more than one kiss was shared." The paper was lying under one of the three benches, held down by a small granite stone. He bent over, picked up the second clue, and read, "A linden by another name would smell as sweet, and this granddaddy overlooks both parking and street." A wave of nostalgia swept over James when he thought of his mother telling him her favorite time of the year was late spring when their giant basswood—linden—was in bloom. And no blossom smelled sweeter or made better honey.

James' childhood home, located near the center of town, had been sold to the city some years before. It was torn down and turned into a parking lot to accommodate the expanding downtown commercial area. But the city council had voted to save the majestic tree, determining it would add both shade and charm to the concrete lot.

It was a short walk from Wide Street to his old home site, and two minutes later James was standing at the base of his mother's beloved tree. He walked to the other side and found the third clue secured with another granite rock. He knelt down, moved the rock aside, and read, "Ash and leather play in the fun, and everyone says there's no place like home." Baseball bats were constructed from ash wood, and gloves were sewn from leather. *Home plate at a ball field is my guess. But which field? Lion's Park by the old elementary school, or one of the newer ones, either at Madison Park or Bobcat High?*

James went with his first guess and trekked up the steepest hill in town to Lion's Park. He stood for a moment recalling all the fun he and Digger and Will had there when they'd played in one of their Little League games, or practiced throwing, catching, and hitting the ball. *Will. Where are you, buddy?* His best friend had last been seen in a café in St. Cloud; he walked out and was never seen again. Another college student gone missing. And no word from him in over thirteen years.

When they found out about Will, Digger cried. James had never seen Digger cry, ever. Not when his mother died, not when his father left, not when his dog died. Will and James had wept like babies when Digger lost his mother and his furry friend, but Digger had just scowled. It had struck James as odd at the time and finally hit him that the only emotion Digger had ever shown up to that point was anger. Not normal.

James realized Digger was never the first to laugh, or even smile, when something good happened to one of the guys. It was like he waited to see how others reacted, then copied them. *Strange*, James had thought at the time, and about a million times since.

Things had never been the same between James and Digger after that. Had Will been the tie that bound them together? Maybe.

Either the clues were easier this year or he was getting better at the hunt. The next clue was half stuck under home plate, with a bigger granite rock to hold down the other side. James pulled out the paper, sat down on the plate, and scanned the field and empty wooden bleachers. He closed his eyes and thought back to the old days when half the town turned out for the games.

Joni, the girl all three of them—Will, Digger, and James—carried a torch for, was always among the spectators, cheering them on. Joni, the cute and spunky little brunette. Joni, the teenager who'd fallen in love with Will, and was crushed beyond belief when he'd vanished. Joni, the woman James had waited for, and welcomed with open arms three years later when she was ready to move on and find love again.

A couple of weeks before their wedding, Digger had pulled James aside and questioned whether it was the right thing to do, marrying Joni. But James had not a single qualm. He loved Joni with every fiber in his being. After they'd married, he finally confessed he had been smitten with her as far back as he could remember. It was something he would have kept to himself had she married Will.

James slapped his thigh and stood up. These clues could have been written especially for him, but it was neither the time, nor the place for a walk down memory lane. Deep breath. Okay. He fingered the paper and focused on the clue. "Under a rock or a family stone, this marker belongs to them alone." Family stone? James pondered the clue for a while, then thought of the two families he knew of in Bobcat that had their surnames etched on large rocks at the ends of their driveways.

He put the sheet of paper back under home plate, jogged to his Ford pickup parked near the village square, got in, and drove to Alvin Johnson's place. No clue had been left under or around his large rock so he got back in his truck and headed to Flanagan's house. The clue was there all right, secured to the ground by a larger granite rock. "The other family stone." James held the paper in his hand for another minute then hit his forehead with the heel of his hand. *It must be the Flanagan's headstone at the cemetery. But what kind of a weird clue is that?* He knew Milt had died a couple of days before and it seemed in poor taste to send medallion hunters to his gravestone. Or, maybe it was meant as a tribute of sorts to him.

James replaced the clue, drove the two miles outside of town to the Memorial Gardens Cemetery, and parked on the road by the entrance. The cemetery was deserted. He remembered there had been a clue left here a few years back, by the headstone of Amasa Oakley, the town's founder. But he had been dead for many years. The elderly Milt Flanagan had just died. For no real reason, a chill trickled down his spine.

James walked around until he located the awaiting grave. The headstone had both of the Flanagan's names, Milton and Shirley, carved into it. The epithet, "United in life, united in death," was true now that Milt had joined Shirley in eternity. James felt like he was intruding when he reached down and retrieved the next clue. "You're almost there." *Almost where?* What in the heck was that supposed to mean?

"Ready to make the journey?" Digger's voice stunned him.

James turned around and thought he was imagining the gun Digger had pointed at him. Then he saw the downright scary, cold-as-ice stare in Digger's eyes and the sneer on his face. "What in the hell are you talking about?"

"The journey into the next life, or at least to the end of this one."

"Put that thing down before someone gets hurt."

"I was thinking dead." Digger waved the gun a hair to the right and back again.

"What has gotten into you? Have you gone crazy?"

"Crazy? Huh. No, I'm completely sane and know exactly what I'm doing. You have something I want. First Will had her, and then it was you."

"Will?"

"I never stood a chance with him around. He had to go. I got elected mayor so I would be her boss. But as long as you're around, she won't let herself fall for me."

"*Joni?* You got elected because you want Joni?" He tried to absorb Digger's words and logic. "That doesn't make any sense. You're not saying you had something to do with Will's disappearance?" An invisible force punched him hard in the stomach.

A satisfied smirk replaced Digger's sneer. "When we got an order to dig a grave back then, the day before Will disappeared, it hit me. The perfect place to hide a body is under another one. I just dug the grave a couple of feet deeper is all."

"I don't believe you." *But deep in his heart he knew it was true. Digger had killed Will.*

Digger shrugged. "Suit yourself." He moved his gun back and forth. "Meantime, jump into your grave."

James took a couple of steps toward Digger. "You say you aren't crazy yet you expect me to jump into that hole?"

"By the time the funeral home delivers the vault and tent, you will be well covered."

"Drop your gun, Digger!" a woman called from nearby.

James was never more relieved to hear his wife's voice.

Digger flinched slightly and threw a quick glance at Joni, one of Bobcat Police Department's finest. She had her service weapon trained on him. "I've come too far to give up now," he spat out.

"Whatever happened, whatever you're talking about, Digger, there's no reason to hurt James. You'd never get away with it."

"I already got away with it thirteen years ago. With Will. He's buried right over there." Digger pointed behind him with his left hand.

Joni struggled to focus as Digger's words sunk in. All the years of wonder, speculation, grief, struggle, and tears. She'd become a police officer because of Will's unsolved disappearance. And he'd been here all along? Her arms went limp and she lost the grip on her firearm. Joni willed her left arm to come to the rescue of her right, but it wouldn't. The Glock fell to the ground and she dropped to her knees behind it like a sack of potatoes.

Digger was distracted by Joni's collapse so James rushed him and grabbed his arm. The gun went off, sending the bullet somewhere out of harm's way. James pushed Digger to the ground and threw himself on top of him. He used every ounce of strength to hold Digger's right arm down as Digger fought against him. Neither James nor Digger realized Joni was back on her feet until she stomped the heel of her hard-soled shoe onto Digger's wrist. His fingers splayed, releasing his grip on the gun.

James jumped up, grabbed the gun, and pointed the barrel at Digger's face. He'd never had the urge to shoot a gun in his life. Until this unreal moment. Joni kicked Digger in the chest with a blow so forceful it rolled him over. A second kick of amazing velocity sent Digger into the open grave.

Joni and James stared at each other, searching the other's face for answers. "He needed to know how it feels," Joni finally said.

James nodded and finished the sentence, "to lie in a grave." He took her in his arms and held her as tight as he ever had. "How did you know what was happening here?"

Joni shivered. "I guess God must have sent me. I was driving by on patrol and saw your truck. I thought maybe you were visiting your Mom's grave, so I pulled in. When I saw Digger holding a gun on you, I honestly thought it was a joke. It took about a split second to realize it wasn't."

A squad car drove down the cemetery lane toward them. "I called for backup and told them to come in silent." Another squad car and fire truck pulled in a moment later. "Digger was Will's friend. Your friend. My friend. What could possibly drive him to kill our dear Will. Or you?"

"Digger is one sick man, Joni." He might tell her more about it someday.

"I know he was never the same after his father ran off when we were seventeen."

"His problems started long before that, and he was a good enough actor to fool us. All of us."

"Poor Will. We need to find out where he is, and do the right thing for him."

A mournful sound made its way out of the open grave. It was the second time in his life James had heard Digger cry. He squeezed Joni's shoulder as the reinforcements ran toward them.

The Sea Horse Swing Ball

Sharon Leah

1973

The waitress shut off the lights behind the counter and approached the table where Xania Maryfield had waited since eight o'clock, the time Roy had said he'd be there. It was nearly midnight. She glanced out the window next to her table. The night was the color of the basalt outcroppings she'd seen along Lake Superior's North Shore, and it was raining.

"I'm sorry, honey. I have to close up in five minutes."

Xania stood. "Thank you for letting me wait here. I really appreciate it."

"Can I call a cab for you?"

"No, thank you. I'll be fine." But as she moved toward the door, she didn't feel fine. She felt afraid and worried that someone had found out about her plan to run away with Roy.

Xania pulled her sweater tighter around her body but the thin material offered no protection from the damp, chilly night. She stood in the pool of weak light from the overhead streetlamp and considered her options. She didn't want to go home or see her mother ever again. Not after she'd threatened to have Roy put in jail after she came home early from bridge club and found them together in Xania's room. Xania had locked herself in her bedroom after Roy left, but she couldn't get away from her mother's accusations.

He's ruined you in the eyes of God and the Church! Her mother had pounded on the door and shouted. *No decent man will have you!*

Xania stepped off the curb and started across Washington Avenue. She heard screeching tires, a car horn blaring, and headlights came to a stop inches from where she stood in the crosswalk. Her heart pounded as the adrenalin rushed through her.

The window on the driver's side rolled down and a man stuck his head out of the opening. "Lady!" the dark-haired man said. "You just walked in front of my car!"

"I'm sorry," Xania said. She couldn't move. Her feet felt rooted to the pavement.

The car door opened. A man got out of the car, rounded the open door, and in two steps was standing in the crosswalk with her. His dark eyes narrowed as he studied her face.

"You're lucky I took some aspirin a while ago and that my knees quit hurtin'. When my knees hurt, I'm not so quick. I could've hit you."

Xania felt the tears coming but she didn't want to cry in front of a stranger. "I'm looking for my boyfriend, Roy," she blurted out.

"Where's he supposed to be?"

Xania nodded toward the darkened diner. "I've been waiting there."

"You don't look like you live around here."

"I don't live here." Xania doubted that anyone lived near the strip joints, adults-only movie theater, bars, pawnshops, auto repair shops, and empty buildings that she'd seen when she walked from the bus stop to the diner. The women wore high heels, not flat shoes like she had on. And their skirts barely covered their butts, unlike the blue skirt she'd worn that was long enough to touch her knees. She clasped her arms tighter across her stomach, because she was cold and because she was aware that her wet sweater was clinging to her small breasts.

"My name's Tony Dufrey." He held out his hand but let it drop to his side when she ignored the gesture. Tony glanced down the street at the cars waiting at the intersection two blocks away for the light to change. "Do you need help? A ride home? I'm a private investigator." Tony got his wallet, opened it, and took out a business card. He held the card out to her.

The signal light turned green and traffic started moving again. "Stay there," he said. "I'm going to turn on my car's emergency flashers.

The approaching cars moved into the right lane and passed them. Only one car slowed down as the people inside stared at them. But no one stopped.

"Come on. Take my card. My name's on it." he said.

She took the card from him. "I have to find him," she said. Her words, when she spoke, sounded slow to her own ears.

"You need to get out of this rain and get warmed up." Tony said. "Let me give you a ride somewhere." He waited a few seconds and then added, "I'll take you anywhere you want to go. You can trust me."

She examined the front and back of the card and let herself believe him. "My name is Xania. Xania Maryfield."

Tony's eyebrows shot up. "Maryfield? Are you related to Robert Maryfield?"

"He's my dad."

Tony strode past her, opened the passenger door, and waited for her. "Come on, Miss Maryfield. Get in," he said. "I'll get a blanket from the trunk." As Tony walked toward the back of his car, he let go a low whistle. "Man! What are the odds that I'd find the daughter of a real estate tycoon in Minneapolis's warehouse district? They're zip. Zilch. Nada."

Xania felt her guard go up. She was used to people treating her differently when they found out Robert Maryfield was her father. But when Tony returned with the blanket, he didn't ask more questions about her father. Instead, he just crouched down and draped the blanket across her shoulders and lap. Then he closed the door. When he was back in the car, he shut off the emergency blinkers and turned the heater knob to high. "Where to?"

"I don't want to go home," she said. "I want to go to South Dakota with Roy and get married."

Tony glanced over at her. "Why not just get married here in Minnesota?"

"Roy isn't Catholic, so we can't get married in the Church." She looked down at her lap. Tears stung her eyes again and she blinked hard to hold them back.

Tony put the car in gear and pressed his foot against the gas pedal. "Well, I have to take you somewhere. Got a relative you can stay with tonight?"

"No. No one," she said as a black and white police car passed them and turned left at the next block. She saw the black and white again in the side mirror as it came up behind Tony's car. "My mother said any children I have with Roy will be bastards and an embarrassment to the Maryfield family."

"That's kinda harsh," Tony said.

"My mother is a harsh woman."

The police car moved into the other lane and passed them again. A moment later, its lights and siren went on. They watched it speed away from them and turn right onto Hennepin Avenue toward the river.

Several more emergency vehicles, sirens blaring, also appeared to be bound for Hennepin Avenue.

"Probably a jumper on the bridge," Tony said. He shook his head and released a deep sigh. "That's such a bad way to die. Way worse than getting hit by a car."

Xania imagined the cold, black water and swift current. "Why would anyone do that?"

Tony shrugged. "People aren't thinking straight when they jump. People need to realize bad stuff happens and get over it." He glanced at her. "Hey," he said, "maybe Roy is trying to call you at home."

The idea that Roy might have tried to call made Xania feel more anxious. He'd be worried because she didn't answer her phone. "Maybe you're right," she said. "I should go home."

"Good plan. Where's home?"

"I live on Lake Harriet Parkway. Do you know where that is?"

"Sure do. I often drive through your neighborhood."

Tony turned right onto Fourth Avenue and followed it to the Interstate 35W exit. Fifteen minutes later, he pulled into the circle drive in front of a three-story Tudor-style home. It was one in the morning and a lot of lights were still on in the house.

Xania opened the door and slid out. "Thank you, Tony."

"Keep my card. Call me if you ever need a PI."

"I'll do that." Xania pushed the door shut and turned toward the house.

❖

The next day, Xania read in the *Minneapolis Star* that an unidentified white male, who was thought to be in his mid-twenties, had fallen from the Hennepin Avenue bridge and drowned. At dinner that night, her father announced that the whole family was leaving in the morning for an extended vacation in Hawaii.

2003

Xania held the sea horse statue and traced its delicate features with her finger. She remembered the day, during the Hawaiian vacation that had stretched from October into December, when she'd bought it. The vacation would probably have lasted longer if she hadn't been pregnant. But when she couldn't hide the pregnancy any longer, they'd flown back to Minnesota. Her father had rented a car at the airport and drove her to a home for girls and unmarried women in Winona. She'd lived there until her baby was born in June.

The pregnancy had been easy and she'd spent many long hours imagining the day she would leave with her baby and go find Roy. But when she awoke after the delivery and was told the umbilical cord had wrapped around her baby's neck and strangled her, Xania's dream died, too. She'd reasoned with herself that life could be cruel, unjust—that she needed to move on.

Xania placed the statue in the box and checked her watch. It was four-thirty. She moved to the stairway and called to her mother, "Are you ready? I'll have to pay the driver for his time and send him home if you don't hurry up. The store closes in one hour."

Elizabeth Maryfield appeared at the top of the stairs wearing a white cashmere jacket. As she descended the steps, she said, "Remind me where we're going."

"We're going to Jillian's Art and Estate Appraisals on Selby Avenue."

"Do we know Jillian?"

"No. But she's collecting items for the Minnesota Zoo's Beastly Ball silent auction. We're donating these items." Xania patted the box with her hand.

"Oh, your father and I attended several of the balls when he was alive. He enjoyed bidding at the auctions, too. One year we bought a trip to New York City."

Xania picked up the box and started toward the door. "Mother, we can talk about the auctions in the car."

"What's the theme of this year's ball?" Elizabeth said. "They always have the best themes."

"It's the Sea Horse Swing. The money collected from the auction will go toward improving the sea horses habitat.

❀

Their driver kept to the middle lane on the freeway, and twenty minutes later he pulled up next to the curb in front of a small shop with yellow window trim and a smart-looking turquoise awning.

"Maybe you can shop while I take care of our donations," Xania said.

Elizabeth leaned forward and looked out the car window. "Nonsense. This is a glorified pawnshop. I'll wait in the car."

"Don't pout, Mother. You're going in with me." Xania got out of the car and waited on the sidewalk for the driver to help Elizabeth from the car.

"We'll be here less than thirty minutes," she said to the driver. "Please park here and wait for us."

Xania found the interior of Jillian's as pleasing as the exterior. Someone had spent a lot of time creating intimate spaces and artful displays. Soft lighting reflected off polished tabletops, elegant pieces of blown glass, graceful Buddha figures, delicate crystal, and China place settings. She turned to her mother and said, "I'm sure you can find something here to look at while I find Jillian."

"Did I hear my name?"

Xania turned to see a slender woman walking toward them from the back of the shop. "I'm Jillian Jackson," she said.

"Hello. I'm Xania Maryfield and this is my mother, Elizabeth Maryfield." Xania tilted her head to one side and looked in the woman's eyes. "Have we met before?"

"Anything is possible. I visit a lot of homes in my business," Jillian said. "What can I help you with today?"

"We have a donation for the Beastly Ball silent auction."

"Oh, wonderful. Thank you! And the animals at the zoo thank you, too," Jillian said. "If you want to set it there," she pointed at a desk that was situated in the center of the shop, "I'll inventory the items for you."

Xania followed Jillian and set the box on the desk. "When I heard it's a sea horse theme for this year, I decided to donate a sea horse I bought in Hawaii over thirty years ago."

Jillian removed the cover and lifted the sea horse out of the box. "It's beautiful!" She turned the statue around slowly and looked at it from all sides before setting it on the desk. "I can't believe you're parting with it. I love sea horses. Do you know that they mate for life?"

Xania laughed. "Yes, and the woman who sold this statue to me also said that sea horses carry the souls of dead sailors to the underworld."

"And that they protect the sailors until they meet their soul's fate," said Jillian. "I've heard that story, too."

"Excuse me for a minute, Jillian. I should check on my mother." Xania left Jillian with the box of donations and walked through the shop until she found Elizabeth looking at a framed painting in one of the displays.

"Xania," Elizabeth whispered, "I think this painting is the one that's missing from my friend Grace's house. Do you suppose whoever stole it brought it here?"

"Mother. I don't think the painting was stolen."

"I'll call Grace when we get home and ask her."

"Okay. You do that." Xania started to leave. "I want to talk with Jillian a little more before we go. Will you be okay?"

"Yes, of course," Elizabeth said. "The criminals won't come back while we're here."

Xania watched her mother begin to examine the lace on a linen tablecloth. "I really like Jillian," she said. "She's like the daughter I used to imagine I would have."

"That's nonsense," Elizabeth said without looking up. "You've only just met the woman."

"I'll be back in five minutes," she said and left Elizabeth sorting through a stack of linens. Xania had hardly opened her mouth to speak when her mother's sharp command silenced her. "Xania. I want to leave—now!" Xania turned to find her mother glaring at her. "Don't just stand there looking dense! We need to go right now. I told you there was nothing in this place for us."

"Mother, you're being rude." Xania glanced back at Jillian. "I'm sorry."

Jillian nodded. "I'll mail the inventory list to you."

Elizabeth was sullen on the ride home and offered no explanation for her outburst. Xania tipped the driver, and when they were inside the house, she said, "Mother, please don't embarrass me like that when I take you out with me."

Elizabeth shrugged off the white cashmere jacket and flung it in a nearby chair. "You've wanted to destroy me, to destroy the family, ever since that summer. You care only about yourself, about what you want!"

"Mother, please calm down," Xania said. "What's making you so angry? She took the cell phone from her jacket pocket and opened Contacts to find the doctor's number. "I'm going to call your doctor and have him come over."

Elizabeth grabbed at Xania's hand and knocked the phone to the floor. "I don't need a doctor!" she shrieked.

"Mother, you're scaring me. I think you're having a stroke or something!" Xania picked up the phone and tried again to find the doctor's number.

"No!" Elizabeth grabbed a metal crucifix from the table and pushed it up toward Xania's face. "Do you see this? I acted in God's name for the good of our family, and now you want to undo everything!" Elizabeth shook the crucifix at her. "I won't allow you to damage our family's name."

Xania was stunned, like the wind had been knocked out of her. She looked at her mother and saw the woman who, in a rage, had beat her the night Tony Dufrey had brought her home. Xania felt afraid. "Mother, what did you do?"

"I got rid of both of them. I made sure that man who got you pregnant could never come back. And I gave that bastard baby of yours to the Church."

Xania felt weak and put a hand on the stair railing to steady herself. "Oh, my god...you killed Roy." Her hands shook as she pushed the button she'd programmed to call 911. When the dispatcher answered, she said, "I want to report a possible murder."

Elizabeth's confession seemed to have turned her anger to fear. She clung to Xania's arm when Xania tried to go up the stairs.

"Please don't let them take me." Xania shook her arm free and left her mother standing alone in the foyer. She went to her old bedroom and knelt by the bed. She felt along the underside of the box-spring frame for the small slit in the fabric. When she found it, she slipped her hand inside and retrieved the newspaper and the business card she'd put there the day they'd left for Hawaii.

When the police arrived, Xania handed over the 1973 *Star* article. "I think this man's name was Roy O'Brien, and he didn't jump from the Hennepin Avenue Bridge. He was killed and she confessed to it." Xania pointed toward Elizabeth.

"You should call your mother's attorney and have him meet us at the station," one of the officers said. "We'll question her there."

Xania called the attorney. Then she called the number on the business card. When Tony DuFrey answered, she said, "This is Xania Maryfield. I'd like you to help me find my daughter."

Corn on the Cob

Colin T. Nelson

Sheriff Todd Simmons vowed to get 'Big John' Hammersmith before the end of his term in office. Simmons returned from a strategy session with the local prosecutor who told Simmons that unfortunately, he couldn't prove Hammersmith guilty—although they both knew he had committed murder.

A month earlier Hammersmith, one of the biggest shake-down men in Sakatah County, had killed Dale Vinkemeier. Dale had worked as an enforcer for Big John, coercing small businesses to pay for "insurance" against fires and damage. Hammersmith killed him in spectacular fashion as a warning to other people who tried to cross him. He gave Dale an overdose of heroin (Dale was an addict) and propped him in the passenger seat of Dale's 1997 Plymouth convertible. Hammersmith then drove the convertible to Dale's home late at night and left him in the driveway for his family to find later. Hammersmith even left a cold six-pack next to the body as a present.

Sheriff Simmons had grown up in the county, graduated from the local high school, and won first place in the state wrestling tournament in the heavyweight division. After attending mechanic's school for two years he'd returned to his hometown. He had a talent for fixing machines, but Todd wanted to do something more important for his hometown. He'd run for sheriff against an incumbent who'd let the county go to hell. Todd had won. Still, the mechanic remained in him and he always carried a toolbox with him for puttering. With only four months left in his term, Todd felt he still had some work left to do, cleaning up the criminal element. It was going to be difficult.

Besides sociopaths like Hammersmith, there were also the small-time crooks that preyed on the local people. Vangie Connors, for instance. A cheap tramp in Todd's opinion, she was a bleached-blond, busty woman who wore tight T-shirts and had a tattoo down her leg that read "Lowell" in remembrance of her boyfriend who now lived in Stillwater Prison. Vangie was a "booster" from the old school.

The manager of Supply Depot complained to Simmons, "She has a specially designed coat, lined with dozens of pockets, and augmented with straps to hold heavier merchandise. When she enters the store, she grabs whatever fits into the pockets of the coat. Our biggest losses are the power tools."

"She probably fences those all over the county," Todd said. "Do you have video of her boosting things? Any proof I could use in court?"

The manager shook his head. "Nope. She's too good. But I'll get her someday."

When Todd got back to his office from his meeting with the prosecutor, his part-time secretary said, "Don't forget about the fundraiser. Sheri Booth called this morning. She's mad as hell."

Todd felt tightness across his back. "Yeah. I'll call her." Booth, president of the Junior Chamber of Commerce, had called about the upcoming Sakatah County Fair. It was the largest fair in southern Minnesota and featured free corn on the cob, served hot in long metal trays. The event had grown to include dozens of other food vendors, live musical entertainment, farm implement displays, and a huge midway with the most up-to-date rides. The chamber depended on revenue from the fair for a big portion of their yearly budget. Todd had volunteered to be the chairman of the fundraiser this year.

He knew it would improve his chances of being re-elected if he beat the dollar goal set last year. But how to do that? Todd wondered.

Of course, he had already talked with every business person in town, met with volunteer groups like the firefighters and Boy Scouts, and had coordinated with every lawyer, banker, and accountant in the county. When Todd added up the pledge numbers, they fell far short of the goal reached the previous year. He had to find a new group of people who would contribute to the cause.

Sheri Booth's voice sounded insistent when Todd returned her call. "Sheriff, you know how important this is to all of us." Her words trailed off as a warning. "And we don't have much time left. You support us and we'll support you."

"I'm working on it," he assured her. When he hung up, the tightness in his back spread to his chest. Holding the office of sheriff of Sakatah County was the best job he'd ever had—and he meant to keep it.

Then, Sheriff Simmons received an emergency call. This time, it was for a dead body at a home in the small town of Union Hill.

"On my way," Todd said. He tightened the brown necktie around his throat, wrapped the belt with his service weapon, cuffs, and speed loaders around his waist, and left for the official car. In the late July heat, the little county seat where Todd worked dozed in the afternoon. Grasshoppers popped out from the dried grass in the parking lot, and when he got into the car, he noticed the heat had made the air smell dusty. The steering wheel burned his fingers.

He turned onto County Road 23, which unrolled straight west until it ran into South Dakota. Along both sides of the road, green corn stretched out in straight rows to the north and south. A breeze lifted the tassels on the plants to make them look like they were growing wispy, yellow hair that hid something below.

Simmons drove past the fairgrounds. At the entrance, an old wooden arch still stood after sixty-seven years. The paint—yellow and green to remind people of the corn theme—probably hadn't been touched up since before his birth. He slowed to glance into the grounds. Dozens of people worked inside. Some moved small kiosks that would be selling greasy food when the fair opened in a week. Another crew rumbled by in large trucks pulling flatbeds behind them. Stacked on the trailers were the unassembled bones of the midway rides. Tilt-A-Whirl, the double Ferris wheel, bungee jumping, and the Bone Shaker—the only one that Todd refused to ride. It used to be called a roller coaster, which had the connotation of some speed—but within reason. The Bone Shaker was designed to scare the crap out of the riders by rising high above the fair and then plummeting to earth as fast as a string of steel cars could fall. At the last second, with only a few feet left before crashing, the cars jerked to the left, corkscrewed 360 degrees, and shot up into the air again like a test pilot trying to break the sound barrier.

He remembered the problem in Union Hill and hurried back onto Highway 23. But he kept thinking about the Bone Shaker. Scary ride.

He activated his siren and called ahead to the county crime lab to meet him at the scene.

When he got to the house, the medical examiner was already there with the local police. An older woman sat in a bench on the front porch. She wore a hot pink halter top, shorts, and a straw snap-brim hat on the back of her head. A hat like Frank Sinatra may have worn. Sweat moistened her forehead, but she didn't look like she was mourning anything.

Todd walked up the steps and introduced himself. He could smell fried bacon from inside the house.

"Candy Monson," she replied. "I own this dump." Her eyebrows bumped up and down. "Can't believe it. In my own house."

"What happened?"

"Uncle Carl lived upstairs for years. We all knew he was kinda different. Hadn't worked on account of his disability. Stayed in his room a lot. We knew he was dealing meth, but what the hell? I didn't care so long as he didn't cause no trouble. And none of his lowlife friends. Couple days ago, this dude came over again. Dontell Green. He went up to Carl's room like usual to buy meth. We didn't think nothing of it. He was up there a long time. One of my kids says she thought she heard a couple a pops. Then, dude comes down and boogies."

"Did you investigate upstairs?" Todd asked her.

She shook her head. "No. Why should we? Then, about three days later, we noticed Carl hadn't come down for any food, so we went up and found him dead. A bullet through the head." Candy took a deep breath. "Didn't smell too good."

"You sure it was Dontell Green?" He sat beside her.

"Who else? Plus he's the only colored dude in the county. Not hard to miss."

"Would you be able to testify about—"

Monson stood abruptly. "Naw. What? One a my kids heard a pop? What the hell would that prove?"

She was right. Without an eyewitness to the shooting or more evidence that Green was the killer, Todd couldn't prove much. Maybe the forensic people would find something. Broken wooden slats on the bench dug into his back and he felt more frustrated than ever. All these criminals were living openly in the county and he couldn't get rid of them.

Two hours later, Simmons returned to his office. A small window air conditioner whined with the effort of cooling the space. His budget had been cut so a new unit was out of the question. Several printed spread sheets about the fundraiser lay across his desk. The numbers looked awful. Plus, he'd already fielded two calls from the media about the death of Carl at the Monson house. Soon, they'd print the story about his failure to "stop" crime in Sakatah County. Two murders in less than two months. Then the TV stations from the Twin Cities would contact him, demanding on-camera interviews. That was the last straw. Todd had to act.

His mind drifted to the county fair. He'd been attending since he was a kid. It had been a long tradition to offer free corn on the cob. The fair even sponsored an eating contest to see who could gobble up the most corn. But unlike everyone else, Todd didn't like corn. Hated it, actually. He pictured the cobs with their rows of yellow kernels that were always crooked.

An idea struck him and he leaned forward in the chair.

If he couldn't prove the cases against the criminals in the county, maybe Todd could at least shake them down for a contribution to the fundraiser. No—the idea was too crazy. He stood up. It wouldn't work. But maybe it would work. They understood that Todd knew of their guilt. Maybe he could threaten them enough to cough up money for the fundraiser.

Of course, it must be done quietly. If the chamber ever knew where some of the money came from…well, he'd be out of office so fast he wouldn't have time to turn off the air conditioner.

The idea grew in his mind as he devised ways to corner the scum of the county. He'd hint that prosecution was inevitable unless they made a contribution. In turn, Todd could offer them free tickets on the rides at the county fair. To an outside observer, it appeared to be a legal trade—contribution money for some rides. No one would ever suspect what Sheriff Simmons had really done to get the money.

The next morning, Todd strolled to the local diner, Neumann's Organic Restaurant—although nothing on the menu was remotely organic. He saw Vangie Connor at the counter in her usual place, as he had hoped to find her. Sitting next to her, he ordered the thin Norwegian coffee and said to Vangie, "How's business?"

Even though it was a no-smoking diner, she finished the last of her cigarette, blew a big lungful of air onto the eggs in front of her, and replied, "What's this about, Sheriff?" She had pale skin, new pimples across her nose, and her hair was still wet from a morning bath. He could smell her floral shampoo.

"I'll get right to the point, Vange. You know I'm facing re-election this fall? I'm starting a crackdown on people like you. I've got a new budget that will fund help from the big boys in Minneapolis to come down with their experts," he lied to her. "I've vowed to get people like you off the streets for good."

Vangie's shoulders shook as she started to laugh. She stopped when she turned to look at Todd. His eyes bored into her and she knew something was different this time. "So, what the hell do you want from me?"

Todd glanced behind them. Two people huddled in a booth on the far side of the diner. He leaned closer to Vangie. "See, I've got another problem. The fundraiser at the county fair needs contributors. Let's make a deal. When the law enforcement from Minneapolis gets here, I'll 'forget' to tell them about you. But I need a generous contribution from you in return."

She ran her hand through her hair and didn't respond for a long time. Finally, she sighed. "How much?"

In five minutes, Todd had his money and had given her free tickets for admission to the county fair and the rides. He left quickly. In the next two days, he managed to round up Big John Hammersmith, Dontell Green, and dozens of other scumbags in the county. Each of them, after some persuasion, had contributed to the fundraiser. Todd gave them all free tickets and warned them to be at the fair on Friday night at eight o'clock—as he would be there watching for them. "To make this look legit, you gotta get on the rides," Sheriff Simmons ordered them all. "I'll be at the Bone Shaker."

By Friday morning, the spreadsheets on Todd's desk looked completely different. He'd not only made the numbers for the goal but had surpassed last year's figures. He took a long lunch and drove out to the fairgrounds late in the afternoon.

The sun glowed through the arch, giving the illusion that the old wood was gilded in gold. The transformation looked magical. He was allowed to drive the official squad car into the grounds. Out of the car, Todd strolled up the dusty street to the corn on the cob booth. He was hungry. He noticed the greasy smell of fried mini-donuts. Shallow trays of butter held endless corncobs, each of them golden as they rolled back and forth in the liquid. Todd selected a hot dog instead, took it from the server, and squirted mustard over it in a long yellow squiggle.

As he started to eat, the attendant for the corn on the cob yelled, "Watch out!"

Todd jumped out of the way as one of the tables buckled from the weight of the corn and collapsed. The tray fell, butter slopped out of the end, and dozens of corncobs bounced off the ground to roll away in dirty trails.

The attendant squatted over the cobs. "Well, we can write their obituaries."

Todd finished his hot dog and walked back to the squad car. He glanced behind him. Three people were watching. "Dog loose," he shouted and hurried to the Bone Shaker as if he were chasing a dog off of a leash—a misdemeanor offense. He ducked underneath the ride and remained hidden in the shadows for a short time.

By eight o'clock, the fair was crowded with hundreds of people. Since there wasn't much else to do in the county, everyone attended the festivities. Todd looked for the "special donors." Had he threatened them enough that they would actually show up? He waited. Ten minutes later, Vangie Connor finally approached the ride carrying a puff of cotton candy on a stick that smelled sweet. She was followed by Big John accompanied by three heavy thugs. Soon, all of the sheriff's "people" were there and had filled the Bone Shaker.

The operator closed the protective railings in each car against all the riders, signaled the other man to start the ride, and the engine chugged into low gear. Metal screeched against metal as the ride came to life. Slowly, the cars clanked up a steep incline. Some people started to scream in anticipation.

The sheriff watched as the cars reached the crest, high in the air, scraped over the edge, and hurtled down toward the ground. The screaming followed the falling cars like smoke trailing from a high-speed locomotive. As the line of cars curled into the 360-degree corkscrew at the bottom, there was a screech of bending steel. Then the rails separated and the cars flew off the ride. They launched into the air, free of any restrictions while the screaming grew to a frightening new level. Then the cars crashed back to the ground, smashing together in an explosion of metal and bodies.

Sheriff Todd Simmons pushed his way through the stunned crowd of people looking at the wreckage. Though he knew it was the scumbags and murderers of the county lying dead amid the rubble, it was still his job to investigate the tragedy and he meant to do his duty. Before he reached the victims, he looked under the ride to make certain he hadn't left any of the tools he'd used earlier behind.

The Missing Groom

Marlene Chabot

The blue and white envelope speckled with purple nosegays came just as I was packing for a weeklong getaway with my widowed aunt to my parents' cabin in the Brainerd Lakes area. From all appearances it looked like a wedding invite, but I couldn't think of a single soul about to tie the knot. The return address didn't help either. I didn't know anyone named Rob Schmidt. Probably a new businessman in town, I thought, as I set it down and went back to packing.

Just as I poked my head in the closet to search for tennis shoes, a loud knock at the door startled me. "Oh crap! It can't be Aunt Zoe. She's not expected for another hour." I left the bedroom, marched to the door and peeked through the peephole. A gal can never be too careful, especially when living in a huge complex like this one. There's no way you can know everyone. Luckily, I recognized the person. It was an old college chum, Karen Foster, with whom I had lost touch several years ago after I got wrapped up in teaching and she in traveling the world. I opened the door.

"Karen! What a surprise! How long has it been?" I asked as I escorted her across the apartment threshold and into the living room. "Three years?"

"More like six." And then the tall blonde threw out her arms and hugged me. I squeezed her back.

When we finished hugging, I stood back and appraised her. "I see you still have your model figure and long, gorgeous hair."

"Knock it off, Mary." Now she carefully studied me. "Looks like teaching little ones has agreed with you. You haven't added a single wrinkle to your forehead."

I laughed. "No, but my hips have become quite impressive." I pointed to the small sleeper couch. "Take a seat." She did as I suggested. Once she was seated, I waltzed over to the La-Z-Boy I had inherited from my brother who was a private eye. "So, what brings you here?"

Karen leaned forward. "I had to come down to the Cities for a fitting and thought I'd look you up."

"What kind of fitting? For work uniforms or a wedding?"

My friend gave me a quizzical stare. "You're joking, right?"

"About what?"

"My fitting. I'm getting married. Didn't you get my invite? I sent it to your folks' address over a month ago and your mom was nice enough to mail it back with your current address."

I scratched my short cropped hair. "I never got it. Unless..."

"Yes?"

"Just a minute." I scooted out of the recliner and went to retrieve the blue and white envelope. When I returned, I handed it to Karen. "I received this today. It's from a Rob Schmidt. I haven't a clue who he is."

"He's my fiancé," Karen proudly announced. "I ran out of labels, so Rob slapped his on. I wonder why the invitation just showed up?"

"It probably ended up in another tenant's mailbox." I took the envelope from my friend and tore it open. "Your wedding's next Saturday?"

Karen beamed. "Ah huh. Do you think you can make it? It's a small, intimate wedding. We just have a best man and a maid of honor."

"How can it be intimate? Fox Run Resort on Bay Lake will be swarming with people. It's their Oktoberfest."

"We know that. Rob proposed at last year's festivities." Karen stood now. "Please say you'll come, Mary. It would mean so much to me if you were there."

"Well, lady, you're in luck. I just happen to be leaving for Brainerd in less than an hour and plan to stay a week."

My friend gave me another hug. "Oh, Mary, it will be so much fun. You'll see."

"Hopefully, the weather will cooperate," I said as I showed her to the door. "This time of year it can put a damper on things."

Karen's excitement followed her across the threshold. "According to the weatherman it's supposed to be a glorious day." She waved and headed towards the elevator.

When she was out of sight, I shut the door and ran to the phone to notify my aunt of a slight change in our vacation plans. Then I flew to the bedroom to pack the appropriate dress and jewelry for an evening, outdoor wedding.

❧

The day after we had settled into the cabin, I began to wrestle with what to purchase for a wedding present. It wasn't so much the gift as it was the dearth of stores. Karen, like me, had been on her own for a long time so I wanted to give her something truly unexpected.

My aunt suggested we drive to downtown Brainerd. A new antique shop had just opened. I liked her idea, so we hopped in the Volkswagen and began our twenty-minute drive to town.

About halfway there, my cell phone buzzed, and I asked my aunt to answer it. "The woman is sobbing," she said. "I can't understand her."

For some reason, I thought of Karen. Maybe the wedding had been called off. I motioned for my aunt to hand me the phone. "Karen, is that you? What's wrong?"

"My maid of honor had emergency surgery this morning," she shared through sobs, "and she'll be laid up for two weeks. Would you be willing to stand up for me?"

Of course I said I would. There's no way I'd let my friend's wedding plans go awry. But now I was expected to give up another evening to attend the groom's dinner as well. As I ended the call, Heavenly Things came into view. "Well, Auntie, let's see if this maid of honor can find the perfect gift."

❖

When Karen informed me of the groom's dinner, she had instructed me to meet Rob and her at 7 p.m. in the lounge at Jerry's Restaurant located on the property of Fox Run Resort. I wasn't thrilled about their choice of restaurants. The annual Oktoberfest events began with the German Buffet on Friday evening at Jerry's. There's no way I'd get to know the groom with a room packed with people singing and swigging overflowing beer steins, but I'd muddle through somehow.

Even though the lounge was unruly and noisy, I was able to pick up a few things about Rob during the dinner. Most importantly, he was attentive to Karen. But tomorrow would be different. He played the tuba for the Blitzer Polka Band from New Ulm and would be performing on and off throughout the day, and that left Karen by herself until the wedding on the shore of Bay Lake. "I wouldn't be so nervous about leaving Karen unattended," he shared, "but two days ago I received a threatening letter from Jill, an old girlfriend."

Karen clenched her beer stein. "You never told me, Rob."

He reached out and cuffed his hand around hers. "You have enough on your plate, sweetheart."

"What did the letter say, Rob?" I inquired in between bites of bratwurst.

"If she couldn't have me, nobody could."

"When did you break up with her?"

"About four years ago, wasn't it?" Karen said.

Rob was trying to sample his plate of Wiener Schnitzel and spargel. "Yes, that's right."

Evidently this woman hasn't learned to get on with her life, I thought. I picked up my glass of Riesling and said, "Look, my brother who's a PI has taught me a few things over the years. Why don't my aunt and I escort Karen around the festivities tomorrow? With two of us guarding her, nothing should happen."

Just then the band started up with Frankie Yankovic's version of "Beer Barrel Polka" and Rob's face broke out in a smile as he sang, "*We've got the blues on the run*... Come on, Karen. Let's dance."

When the couple left, Rob's best man, Clyde, took off for a beer refill, and I ignored my diet and went straight to the dessert table to scoop up a huge portion of apple strudel. Tomorrow I would suffer the consequences.

❧

The next morning, I opened my eyes to find Aunt Zoe standing over me lecturing me about something. I ignored her and glanced at the bedside clock instead. Oh no! 7:45. Karen was expecting us at nine. "Mary, why bother telling me you wanted to be awakened two hours before we're expected at Fox Run if you're not going to get up? Last night you said you needed to shower, wrap your gift, and stop for gas."

I jumped out of bed and on the way to the shower begged my aunt to slap a bow on my gift.

After I finished dressing, the two of us took one final look at each other's appearances. Tons of men would be milling about at Fox Run Resort and we both hoped to catch a single man's fancy, even if we were involved in a private wedding later in the day. "I think we look ravishing, Auntie."

"Ah huh. Let's go."

On the way to the resort, I quickly explained Rob's fears regarding Karen's safety. "I don't foresee a problem at breakfast. What I'm concerned about is the rest of the day."

"Why?"

"Karen wants to hit all the craft and art booths before the entertainment starts, and then follow Rob as his band moves from tent to tent."

Auntie, never having attended an Oktoberfest, said, "That doesn't sound dangerous to me."

"There's tons of ground to cover," I said. "Sixty booths outside and at least that many inside. And when the weather's great, like today, shoppers act like it's Black Friday. Entertainment in the tents is the pits too. One can barely squeeze into one, let alone find an empty seat."

Aunt Zoe continued to watch the scenery. "We'll have to pretend we have superglue on, Mary, and cling to each other like flies. Oh, there's the sign for the Oktoberfest up ahead. A young fellow's already out directing traffic."

"Good."

❀

"Am I glad to see you," Karen said, as my aunt and I slid into her booth at the lodge's Moose Café. "I almost thought our wedding was going to be cancelled."

Aunt Zoe opened her menu and stared at it. "Wedding jitters?"

"No, it's not that. Rod swears he saw Jill while we were dancing last night and then I did something unthinkable this morning. I left our room to get us coffee while Rob was in the shower."

A teenage waitress swooped in, deposited three glasses of water and took our orders for coffee, wild rice pancakes, and sausage.

After she left, I returned to Karen's story. "I suppose Rob went ballistic when he didn't find a note?"

"You got it."

"Well, you can't blame him. He's taken that threatening letter to heart. Now listen, Karen, I know you want to visit all the vendors, but you have to stay focused and be aware of what's happening around you."

Aunt Zoe set her water aside. "Did Rob ever show you a picture of his old girlfriend?"

"Yes. Jill's picture was in the newspaper last year when she received a real estate award."

I grabbed my black clutch purse and whipped out paper and pen. "Describe her for us."

"She has hazel eyes, medium-length naturally wavy black hair, and is close to your build, Mary. Oh, and she wears tortoise shell glasses."

"Height?"

"Rob said five foot four."

The minute breakfast ended, we walked to the lodge's second floor to see the craft displays. It wasn't until we entered the third room filled with candles, jewelry, paintings, and scarves that a minor incident occurred involving my friend. A woman rushed Karen. We tried to fend her off, but didn't succeed. She already had her arms wrapped around Karen. "You're not going anywhere!" the woman screamed.

I studied the overwrought woman's features. It wasn't Jill, but I still wasn't going to allow anyone to terrorize my friend on her wedding day. I began to peel one of her arms off of my friend. "Leave Karen alone."

The unknown assailant immediately released her grip. "Her name's Karen?"

"That's right," Aunt Zoe said as she moved in behind her.

"I'm sorry. I didn't mean to scare you," the fifty-something woman said to Karen. "You look like the gal who's been fooling around with my husband."

My friend was a bit shaken, but she graciously accepted the apology and said we should move on; we still had five more rooms to stroll through before we could even think about going outside to see the other vendors and the bands.

Luckily, morning slipped by without another incident. It was now noon, and we decided to drop our shopping bags in Karen and Rob's room before we went off to get a bite to eat and listen to Rob's band.

When we entered the room, Karen noticed a small package wrapped in wedding paper sitting on the desk. "Is that from you gals?"

"Nope," I replied. "Read the card."

She picked it up. "That's odd. It just says 'Wish you well.' No signature." She dropped the card back on the desk before moving towards the door to leave. "Maybe Rob will recognize the handwriting."

The Blitzer Polka band was just getting situated as we entered the larger of the two tents. It was a huge group consisting of musicians and singers. Rob managed to give Karen a quick wave. She waved back. "Aren't the men adorable in those red and black suspenders, and their lederhosen shorts?"

"Personally," I said, "I prefer a man in a tux."

Karen laughed.

The band started up finally, and Aunt Zoe leaned over and whispered in my ear, "I hope they play, 'I've Got A Wife.' It's my favorite." To her disappointment the first tune was "Hoop-Dee-Doo."

When the band broke into their sixth song, "Who Stole the Keeshka?" the Narrens, masked characters dressed in German village folk costumes, filed into the tent and snaked their way around the crowd. Everyone began to clap to the music as this person and that were dragged from their seats to dance with one of them. I was sweating bullets, hoping I wouldn't be taken away from my security duties. It didn't matter. Karen got swept up instead.

My aunt frowned. "Now what? How do we guard her from here?"

"Just keep your eagle eyes on her."

The minute the song was over, the female Narren who had borrowed our bride-to-be returned her to us, and whispered in her ear. Then she trotted off to wait for the next dance. "That was quite a work out," my friend shared as she clutched her side. "I could use a glass of wine."

"I'll get it. Do you want anything, Auntie?"

"Strudel with ice cream."

Even though I was pleased nothing had happened to my friend while she was dancing, I thought it strange Jill had not taken advantage of the situation. If she wanted to cause bodily harm to Karen, she missed the perfect opportunity. Maybe Rob misunderstood the letter. What if she meant to harm *him*? I stood. "Karen, when you circled the crowd, did you see anyone who resembled Jill?"

"Sorry. Everything was a blur."

"That's okay. I'll scan the crowd."

When I returned to the tent, I found Aunt Zoe and Karen giggling hysterically. "What's so funny, you two?" I queried as I handed the wine and dessert off.

"Oh, Mary," Karen said, "You should have seen Rob. A Narren grabbed him off the stage and they danced to the "Pennsylvania Polka" right in front of us. He acted so awkward. It was hilarious."

I glanced at the stage. No Rob. Alarms blasted through my head. "Where's Rob?"

"Probably getting a drink to cool off," Karen said.

Aunt Zoe acted annoyed. "Can't the man take a break, Mary?"

"Sure, but the music sounds better with his tuba. Say Karen, what did the Narren whisper in your ear?"

"She was going to get my boyfriend later. I presumed she meant to dance. Why?"

"No reason," I lied. I wasn't prepared to share my worries with Karen yet, but if Rob wasn't back on stage in another five minutes I'd be forced to. I kept an eye on my watch.

❀

The deadline came and still no Rob. It was time to take action. "Karen, which Narren danced with Rob?"

"The same one I danced with."

"The old humpbacked woman?"

"Yeah."

"She had bright red shoes," Aunt Zoe added, "and a long pointy nose."

I jumped up and grabbed both gal's arms. "We need to search for Rob."

"Why?" Karen asked as we exited the tent.

"He's been kidnapped."

My friend began to cry. I placed an arm on her shoulder. "We'll find him. Auntie, you search the booths out here. Karen, check the lodge. I'll cover the rest of the outdoor area. Meet back here in an hour."

"That's when our nuptials are scheduled," Karen blubbered.

"I know."

With only ten minutes to spare, I discovered where Jill had secretly stashed Rob. Seeing the large wishing well by the lodge clicked things into place. The note in the room. *Wish them well.* Jill subconsciously gave her plan away. A stranger and I hoisted out the bound and gagged Rob. He rushed off to change. I called the gals. "Karen, get your gown on. Then meet us by the lake. The wedding's on."

After the brief ceremony, I presented my gift. "You can return it if you want. I'd understand."

"No way," the happy couple chimed. "The wishing well will remind us of our wedding day."

"And the missing groom," I quipped.

"So, did the police catch Jill?" Aunt Zoe asked when Rob and Karen left to dance.

"Yup. Jill said she only hid Rob so Karen would think he left her at the altar. Crazy woman."

The Wooden Boat Show

Michael Kelberer

Ivar Torgelson stood on the bluff facing Lake Superior and pulled his overcoat tighter against the stiff May breeze blowing inland. Arrayed below him were the buildings, docks, and work areas that were his kingdom: the Swensen & Torgelsen Marina and Boat Works. Everything was shiny, modern, efficient, and very prosperous. The only part of the view that Ivar didn't enjoy was the word "Swensen" still on the sign. His grandfather had left it there as part of his public relations defense against the rumors of foul play surrounding the original Swensen's death and Torgelson's consequent acquisition of the business. Two generations later, the marina had grown into the dominant boat business on Lake Superior's North Shore.

A sudden gust of wind brought Ivar back to the present. It had been a good run, but the business had reached its peak some years ago. It was time to cash out.

On advice of his attorney, he was withholding the announcement of the sale until after this weekend's annual Wooden Boat Show and Charity Auction. It was the marina's signature public relations event, and a successful one would, his attorney said, add to its perceived value. The marketplace for such a business was uncertain at best, and they would need every edge they could get.

The Wooden Boat Show opened the next morning, Friday, and already the marina's large landing area below him was humming with artisans and craftsmen setting up their stands, stalls, and tents. There was an unusually large number of them this year—Melissa, a new event organizer from the Twin Cities he had hired, was clearly earning her keep. He spotted her talking to a young woman with a professional-looking video camera filming a shoemaker setting up shop. That was new, too. On the north end, several polished and gleaming wooden boats were being maneuvered into display positions in the center square, or being pushed into the large boat shed for storage until Saturday's Charity Auction. The auction was a boat show favorite, with proceeds going to the local Tamarack Foundation, something his attorney would talk up with potential buyers.

Ivar saw a volunteer removing a tarp from the last boat entering the shed—and Ivar was shocked to see it was a dilapidated old Chris-Craft cruiser with, it appeared, some serious hull damage. Not a chance, he thought, and hurried down the wooden stairway to the landing, calling his event organizer as he went.

By the time he reached the shed, she was waiting for him.

"Melissa, what is this?"

"You saw the Chris-Craft," she said, meeting his eyes serenely. "I know it's unusual, but the owner insists it will fetch an excellent price—in fact he's guaranteed a minimum donation to the foundation regardless of the bidding."

"But we haven't had time to—"

"I have a notarized proof of ownership," Melissa said. "Besides, Jon Swensen is very persuasive."

Ivar started at the name. "I don't believe I've met a Jon Swensen. Is he from Tamarack?"

"Here he comes now," said Melissa, and walked away briskly.

A tall, blond man in an expensive three-piece suit was approaching with a wide smile and an outstretched hand.

"Mister Torgelson, my name is Jon Swensen, and I want to thank you for taking my boat at the last minute."

Ivar released his hand, studying his face. There was something... "Well, I haven't taken it yet Mr. Swensen. Have we met before?"

"Call me Jon, and I don't believe we've had the pleasure, Ivar."

"Hmm." Ivar gestured at the other boats. "As you can see, we only take new or fully restored boats for the auction."

"You might want to make an exception in this case, Ivar. This one will get some serious interest. You see, I've shown it to an expert...actually, here he is. I'll let him tell you."

Ivar turned and saw a large, burly man dressed in Carhartt apparel and work boots. He was sporting a Boat Show Participant badge on his breast pocket.

"Ivar, let me introduce you to Fred."

"Are you a boat builder or appraiser then, Mister...?"

"Just Fred, please. And yes, but this is my first year up here on the

North Shore. Two interesting things about this boat, Mr. Torgelson. One, the interior has some classic smuggler modifications. Judging by its age, I'll bet it was used to run whisky during Prohibition."

As he talked, Fred was making his way around the boat. Ivar followed, not liking what was developing. First, the name Swensen, and now this talk of smuggling.

"And, second, take a look at the hull damage," Fred continued. "All the boards are bent outward. That's no reef damage—this boat was deliberately scuttled."

Swensen jumped in. "Great story, eh, Ivar? Sure to attract some hefty bids, damaged or not. Also, there's a name on the back—we might even be able to get some specifics by the time the auction starts tomorrow."

Ivar had reached the boat's stern. The nameplate was partially defaced with age and use, but he could read it: the Eastern Express. He threw a sharp glance at Swensen, whose smile was unchanged. So that's why his face looked familiar—it reminded Ivar of the portrait of old Albert Swensen that hung in the marina's office. Ivar shivered, but quickly composed himself. It was probably just a bit of basic extortion. He could deal with that. Time to test the price.

"We really can't take such a boat for our auction, Mr. Swensen, but I appreciate your generosity and hate to see you go away empty-handed."

He paused, but Swensen's face gave away nothing.

"Why don't I take this boat off your hands and have my company restore it. I'll donate the sale price—shall we say $35,000?—to the Tamarack Foundation and add a $10,000 finder's fee for your trouble. Win-win wouldn't you say?"

"Well, Ivar, that's very generous of you. But I'm a big believer in the free marketplace and if you don't want it in your auction, I certainly understand, but in that case I would just hold my own auction up on Main Street. You want me to have it removed?"

The smile had returned, but behind it the eyes had gone steely. More than just a simple bit of extortion then. Round one to Swensen, who doubtless knew Ivar would not let this particular boat out of his sight.

"Perhaps I'm being a little too conservative, Mr. Swensen. Let me think on it and I'll let you know later this afternoon."

Still the smile, another friendly handshake, and Swensen and Fred left.

✿

Ivar locked the shed from the inside, loosened his tie and sat down heavily on a handy hard-backed chair. The Eastern Express. Definitely the boat his grandfather's partner had perished in. The official story had involved a terrific storm, a foolhardy rum-running jaunt, and an unfortunate encounter with an unmarked rock reef. Outwardly, his grandfather had grieved, placed a new, lighted buoy on the reef, paid for a major funeral, and left his partner's name in the marina's name. Meanwhile, he had used every lever of wealth and intimidation at his disposal to quash the investigation (not difficult since the boat had never been found) and defeat the Swensen's lawsuit.

Facing Swensen in the boat shed, Ivar had felt some moments of anxiety, but his mind was clearing and he examined the alternatives.

Could Swensen be contemplating legal action, with this morning's charade simply a ploy to get Ivar off his guard? Perhaps, but that didn't seem likely. Yes, the Eastern Express had clearly been scuttled, putting the lie to the "unmarked reef" story. But how could they prove who had done it? Ivar couldn't imagine any DNA or other evidence having survived the storm. Still, a lawsuit would be most inconvenient now.

Ivar shook his head. That didn't feel right. Maybe Swensen was just trying to reopen the case in the court of public opinion, to humiliate him in front of the town of Tamarack during the marina's (and therefore Ivar's) most public event of the year. If his pride were the only consideration, Ivar could simply call his bluff: accept the boat, let it go up for auction, and let the townspeople have their fun. The marina was the town's biggest employer—he would use the same combination of public denial and private blackmail to ensure the controversy would be no more than a seven-day wonder.

Unfortunately, his local honor was not all that was at stake. The real problem was that the re-appearance of the boat itself, especially at the Boat Show, would generate a statewide media feeding frenzy—"Rum Runners," "Betrayal," "The Mighty are Falling"—that, realistically, would crater his attempts to sell the business. Buyers would worry that the negative publicity would permanently drive away customers. They might even worry the Swensen family could void his title to the business.

He stared at the boat. What would his grandfather have done? After a few minutes, the beginnings of a solution came to his mind, and a smile spread on his face. He simply had to remember that the overall goal was not reputation management itself, but to cash out. Perhaps Swensen's appearance, rather than creating a new problem, could become the solution to an old one. His attorney had repeatedly warned him that a speedy outcome from the sale was far from assured. And uncertainties in the marketplace for large businesses, along with the recent recession, made future proceeds almost impossible to estimate.

Insurance proceeds, on the other hand, with the right story and tactics, could be quick and final.

He stood up, straightened his tie, and went to find Swensen.

❀

Late that evening, Ivar was in the boat shed emptying his last can of gasoline into the Eastern Express. Other cans stood at strategic points around the premises with trails of gasoline leading back to the boat.

He glanced at his watch; nearly time for Swensen to arrive.

No way to hide the arson, of course. But, like his grandfather before him, he had the means to control the investigation. On the legal side, most of the local authorities had attained office based on his sizable campaign contributions. And his local, independent insurance company had gotten rich from his family's business over the years. What they would need was a credible perpetrator not named Torgelson, and Swensen, with his public attempt to intimidate Ivar, would be perfect: "Swensen heir returns to Tamarack to avenge grandfather's alleged wrongful death, but dies carelessly in the attempt." The story would give the authorities and his insurance agent what they needed, especially with Melissa and that guy Fred to corroborate it.

Ivar smiled. It was such an elegant solution.

He heard a crunching in the gravel leading up to the shed's side door. He quickly pulled a revolver out of his belt and turned off the lights. He didn't want to give Swensen any time for heroics.

The door creaked open. "Hello?" It was Swenson's voice.

Ivar aimed the pistol in the direction of the door, and turned on a light.

"Good of you to come, Mr. Swensen. Please step this way."

Swenson's face broadened into that damnable smile as he walked into the circle of light.

"Well Ivar, it appears this meeting is not quite as advertised. I'm betting you're on to my little secret."

"Stop there please. Just out of curiosity, what did you expect to get out of all this anyway?"

"Why, justice, Ivar. Simple justice. Your grandfather killed my grandfather and stole our family's fortunes. I can't abide that."

"Justice, Mr. Swensen? Seems more like simple revenge to me."

Swensen pointed to the gasoline cans. "Planning a party?"

"Why yes. And you're the guest of honor." Ivar, feeling expansive, gestured with the pistol. "Move over here beside your boat, Swensen. Seems fitting, doesn't it? I'll kill you in the same place my grandfather killed yours."

"Ah, so you admit it. Well, thank you, Ivar, that's pretty much the icing on the cake."

Ivar suddenly realized that Swensen seemed not at all worried.

"What cake?"

Swenson's smile got wider.

"You see, Ivar, we would have settled for simply scuttling your attempt to sell the business. But when you invited me to a late night meeting, we realized you would probably hand us a much sweeter opportunity. And you have."

Ivar had just time to wonder, "We?" before he received a sharp blow to the head.

❀

Ivar's next awareness was the pounding in his head. Then he realized that he was seated in a hard-backed chair with his arms and legs tied. He opened his eyes. The light from just one of the overheads created a narrow cone of illumination with a small table at its center. On the table was a thick legal-looking document. Across the table, Swensen stood next to two men, and Ivar was startled by the fact that he recognized one of them.

"Welcome back, Ivar," Swensen said. "Fred's last name is Swensen and he's my nephew. The other gentleman is Jeff Anderson, my son-in law."

Ivar felt his stomach start to sink. His head was still pounding and he was having trouble getting his thoughts around what was happening. Three Swensens? Clearly he had been set up. But for what?

Another person stepped forward into the light. Melissa!

"And Melissa Smith, nee Swensen, my sister and an excellent event organizer, wouldn't you say?"

Ivar remembered the unusual bustle of activity that morning, and his stomach sank further. Were they all Swensens?

"Justice, Ivar," said a new voice, and another figure emerged into the circle of light—his business attorney!

"David Christie," said Swensen, "who's my uncle by the way, has modified your sales documents to confer all of your assets to the Swensen Family Trust." He gestured to the paper pile on the table, and Ivar saw there was a signature page on top. "Sign it, and we'll let you slink out of Tamarack with the cash in your bank account."

The direct threat awakened Ivar's pride. "I will do no such thing. You can't prove a thing. Tell your story and be damned. I'll just wait for the publicity to blow over."

"Ah, but it's not just bad publicity you should be worried about, Ivar." Another person stepped forward into the light, the young video photographer he'd seen that morning. Ivar felt outnumbered, outmaneuvered, overwhelmed.

"Meet my sister Elizabeth," said Swensen, "master of all things video. When she gets done with the recordings from your security cameras, you'll be looking at five-to-ten for attempted sabotage and attempted murder."

The smile had left Swenson's face as he was talking and Ivar saw the hard, cruel lines that had been so carefully hidden behind it. Fred walked over, freed his arms, and handed him a pen.

"So much simpler for both of us, though, if you just sign. So we'll sweeten the deal—we'll leave the video behind."

Ivar took a deep breath. He must remain calm. Clearly, his first priority was to get the Swensens out of there. Afterwards, he'd claim duress and tie up the Swensens in court. Then the new Swensen would have to learn the old Swensen's lesson: you don't stand in the way of a Torgelson and survive. He reached over and signed the document.

Swensen gave a satisfied nod, and then turned to the others and said, "Let him go."

Fred and Jeff reached behind Ivar, and he could feel his remaining bonds loosening. Ivar felt a great sense of relief, and his mind started kicking into gear. They walked past him toward the back of the shed. Ivar stood up to watch them, and was already planning his first phone calls, when they all stopped and turned to face him. Swensen called "Now!"

Ivar felt someone moving behind him. Strong hands seized his arms and spun him around. Someone flipped a light switch, illuminating the front half of the shed.

Ivar drew a sharp breath, and for the first time he could remember, he felt real fear. Before him was a noose dangling from a rafter, and underneath it, another of the hard-backed chairs.

❁

Jon Swensen and the others were gathered at the top of the cliff, along with hundreds of townspeople, gazing down at the marina. Word of the excitement at the marina had spread quickly.

The EMT's had taken Ivar's body away some hours ago. Fred, who had arrived at the marina early, ostensibly to finish setting up his booth, had "discovered" the body and extinguished the fire before much damage had been done. He'd been interrogated and, as planned, had pointed the finger at Jon, "I'm pretty sure there was something between them." Jon was found, and admitted that he had confronted Torgelson about the boat and the threat of exposure, inducing him to sign over the marina. He'd left Torgelson understandably disconsolate, but alive. He'd shown the sheriff the signed agreement, with its damning set of initial stipulations that Ivar hadn't bothered to read. Jon agreed with the sheriff—the document was as good as a suicide note. As a seeming afterthought, Jon mentioned the security cameras. Surely they would back up his story. The sheriff seemed to buy it, and had let Jon go with the admonishment to "not leave town."

Jon smiled at the memory. He was here to stay. Elizabeth's carefully edited version of the security video would show an Ivar Torgelson confessing his grandfather's sins, starting the fire, and hanging himself. There would be no evidence in the video of two Swensen nephews who had "assisted" Ivar in his final moments.

Jon noticed Fred looking at the massive sign atop the marina, smiling.

"Yep," Jon said, "I think it might be finally time for a name change."

All Sales Final

Douglas Dorow

"Come on, Carter. We've got some ground to cover. The hunt is on."
Friends since elementary school, Carter and I had survived high
school and the streets of Chicago. Summers, we'd worked for Carter's
uncle in his antique store where I picked up knowledge of antiques and
collectibles. Carter pursued the artistic talents he'd inherited from his
mother and honed in her studio. Turning twenty-six, we'd pooled our re-
sources and opened an art gallery and antique store in the Pilsen neighborhood on Chicago's Lower West Side.

Now our summers were spent touring the Midwest, stopping at art
fairs, auctions, and festivals in search of treasures to resell in our gallery.

"You have the cash?" I asked.

Carter tapped his pocket. "Right here, Bobby. Twenty big ones."

"Well, be careful with it. Let's go see if we can spend a little." I led
the way through the crowds. Carter followed. The warm sun on a late
July weekend brought people out of their homes and into town from
their lake cabins to mingle and look for treasures at Pelican Rapids'
craft and art festival—*Art in the Park*. We bumped our way through the
crowds from the parking lot past the food vendors. Turkey legs smoked
over the long, brick grill pits. People lined up to buy a plate of shredded
turkey on a bun, chips, and a pickle. Carter wanted to stop but I kept
moving forward.

I scanned the booths, the tables under the pop-up tents and cano-
pies that lined both sides of the walking trails through the park. Craft
and art festival? I didn't see much art. It was mostly crafts, knick-knacks,
and food. But we'd found treasures in these Midwest festivals before.
Today might be our lucky day.

Carter caught up with me and held out a bag filled with mini-
donuts. "You want one?"

"No. How can you eat those things?"

"They help the hangover," Carter answered, sugar crystals flying out of his mouth as he spoke. "And I need the energy. My legs are a little tired after that street dance last night. These farm girls can dance." He did a little two-step with a spin as we walked.

I couldn't help but smile. I don't know what it is, but Carter charms the women. He was dressed like a wise-guy: white shoes and black ankle socks with fat, hairy legs running up to baggy plaid shorts, short-sleeved shirt, untucked, hugging his protruding belly. The top three buttons of his shirt were open, exposing his hairy chest and the gold chain hanging around his neck. Atop his round head balanced a small black straw fedora with a white ribbon around it. "Is that what you wore?" I asked.

"More or less. Something wrong with it?"

"You kind of stand out."

"Ex*cuuu*se me," Carter said. "You don't really blend in either with your custom clothes, gold ear studs, and leather slides. Look around you. We're in Pelican friggin' Rapids, home of turkey farmers and weekend fishermen."

"Let's get busy. I'll take this side, you take the other," I said.

"Forget these trinkets. Follow me down to where the *arteests* hang out." Carter held out his bag of mini-donuts to tempt me to follow.

The "arteests," as Carter called them, were in a flat semi-circular grassy area bordered on one side by the old millpond. We split up to scour the booths and paintings; Carter went left, I went right.

❂

I was admiring some small oil paintings of loons and swans when Carter grabbed me by the arm and pulled me over to a tree. He had a double-scoop ice cream cone in his other hand.

"What's up?" I asked. "Did you get me one?"

"One what?" Carter asked.

I nodded at the ice cream cone.

"No." He shook his head. "Now listen." Carter took off his fedora, wedged it under the arm holding the ice cream cone, took a big lick and wiped the sweat off the top of his head. "While you were in there browsing the pretty little bird paintings that we could never sell, I wandered over to the tents by the pond. There are some artists painting the park and the suspension bridge."

"Are they that good?"

"What?" Carter asked with a confused look on his face.

"You want a painting of the bridge? Think we can sell it?"

"Shut up." Carter punched me in the arm. "Just listen."

"You hit me?" I started laughing. "You haven't hit me since we fought over Jan Macdonald in eighth grade."

"I'll hit you again if you don't shut up." Carter made a fist and slowly drew back his arm.

I put up my hands, giving up. "You win. I'm done talking."

Carter shifted from foot to foot, unable to stand still. He started talking with his hands, waving the ice cream cone in the air before the words came out of his mouth. "OK. I was over there looking at paintings on display and watching some of the artists paint. I looked over the shoulder of one old lady painting a lousy landscape of the bridge."

I raised my eyebrows and twirled my hand, urging Carter to speed up, to get to the point.

Carter slapped my hand down. "I'm getting there." He inhaled deeply and exhaled in a blast. "This old lady was painting over a canvas that had something on it. It looked like a Civil War sketch."

Carter was looking at me like he was waiting for a response. "And I guess that's special," I said.

"Yes, that's special. Haven't you learned anything over the years about art?" Carter started walking away, paused and looked back over his shoulder. "You coming?"

Carter walked past the first artists straight to an old, white-haired lady wearing a straw hat under a faded green beach umbrella, and stood behind her. I lagged behind him. When I caught up, he turned and whispered, "This is it."

We stood behind her and watched her paint. The painting wasn't that lousy. She had some skill, an eye for detail. That was apparent. Her hands were a little shaky, but with determination and an elastic brace on her wrist for support and strength, she painted the millpond in front of her. Three quarters of the canvas was covered with her work in progress. The lower right quarter was still uncovered. Visible in that quarter were some sketch lines. They didn't match the rest of the picture. I moved around to the right behind her and tried to get a better look at the sketch.

Carter stepped around her left side and watched her paint. "You have an excellent eye."

"Thank you," she answered, without taking her eye from the canvas. She finished her stroke, sat back, set down her brush, and massaged her right hand with her left. "*Uff da*. I need a rest." She removed her glasses, put on her over-sized sunglasses and looked at us. "So, you boys like art?"

"I studied art a little in school. Where are my manners?" Carter held out his hand and gently shook the woman's hand. "I'm Carter, and my friend here is Bobby. We're vacationing at a resort here and thought we'd experience the art fair."

"I'm Lois." She pointed with a shaky hand towards one of the booths. "I'm here with my sister, Hilda."

"Well, Lois." Carter walked over to the painting and looked it over. "You have great technique."

"I've been painting a long time."

I had to ask. "Lois, what's this in the corner you haven't painted yet?" From what I could see it looked like a sketch of a battle scene. An old scene, muskets and sabers old.

"I reuse old canvases. That's just something that was on there." Lois started to get up. "Can I show you boys some of our other paintings? And you can meet my sister."

Carter stepped forward and gave Lois his arm, and walked her back to her booth over the uneven grass. I hung back and looked at the painting, focusing on the sketch in the corner. Up close the soldiers, flags, muskets, and landscape stood out. It appeared to be an old Civil War battle scene. I touched the edge of the frame to feel the canvas and walked around to glance at the backside for any markings or signatures. I didn't know what we'd stumbled on here, but I hustled over to the tent to see what else we could learn from the sisters.

❀

"Here's Bobby. Let me introduce you." Carter stepped aside and introduced me to Hilda. She and Lois were definitely sisters. Both had gray hair, glasses, and the same smile. I shook Hilda's hand, a light grasp in my own to protect her frail, bent fingers.

"Nice to meet you, Bobby. Can I get you something cold to drink?"

Carter held up a bottle of beer glistening with condensation from the hot, humid day. He'd finished his ice cream cone.

"Thank you. I'll have what he's drinking."

Hilda laughed and handed me two bottles and a bottle opener. "Can you open one for each of us? I think I'll join you."

"Lois, how about you?" I asked.

Lois sat in a chair and waved a hand. "None for her," Hilda added. "She's a wine drinker." She poured red wine into a plastic glass and brought it to Lois.

Carter examined the paintings that hung from the walls of the tent. There were scenes of Pelican Rapids and what I suspected were small towns and farms from the area. "How are sales, ladies?" he asked.

"It's early, so it's a little slow." Hilda said. "Things will pick up. See anything you like?"

"Hilda, I believe you are a salesperson. If you're in Chicago and want a job, you can work in our shop."

"You're from Chicago?" she asked.

Carter kept talking. "Yeah, we have a small business in Chicago. We have a little gallery where we sell art and antiques. We use some of our vacation to visit the Midwest for items to buy if we think we can find a buyer for them."

I had to jump in. "I think you have some things we'd be interested in. Some of our customers like the cute, small town scenes."

"Lois, these boys are from Chicago. How about that?" Hilda said.

"Yes, I know. The Windy City."

Hilda sat in the chair next to Lois. "I'm sorry boys. I need to sit. It's going to be a long day." She gestured towards a couple of other chairs in the tent. "Sit, let's talk and have another beverage."

Carter sat across from Hilda, a fresh beer in his hand. Hilda was still nursing hers and I had a fresh one in hand as well. "It's interesting you're from Chicago. That's where our family's art background started," Hilda said.

"Really?" Carter asked. "Your family's from Chicago?"

"Oh, no," Hilda laughed. "We're Otter Tail County people through and through. Both Lois and I married local boys and outlived them."

"Maybe because we're not teetotalers." Lois laughed and took a sip of her wine. "It was our great grandfather who went to Chicago. The family story is that he wanted to sign up for the Civil War, but he was sixteen and had some artistic talent, so they shipped him to Chicago to apprentice with an artist who was documenting the war for the *Chicago Tribune.*"

That got my attention. I glanced at Carter and leaned forward in my chair. "Seems like the talent continued through the bloodline. You have some talent, Lois."

"Yes, my little sister has always been good at drawing or painting, ever since we were little girls," Hilda replied. She reached over and gave Lois's hand a squeeze. "Our parents sent us both off to college. Lois studied art; I was a stewardess for a while and then came home to be a history teacher. Papa could paint...barns." She and Lois both laughed. "He recognized our talent and interests and sent us off to school to get educated. A chance to get off the farm."

"So, these canvases Lois is painting on came from your great grand-father?" Carter asked.

"Yes, he came back from Chicago with all sorts of sketches on can-vases and old rolls of canvas. I think it was either what the paper didn't want or what he drew that wasn't good enough. And we're trying to supplement our income, so rather than buy new canvases to paint on, we recycle. Don't want to waste anything."

Carter looked around at the paintings hanging in their booth. "All these are painted over old canvases?"

"Yes, the canvas that was in good enough condition," Hilda said.

"And you have some old canvas here she hasn't painted yet?"

Hilda pointed to a wooden box under the tent. "Lois has the can-vases she picked out to paint on in there."

Carter got up, strode over to the box, and pulled out a stretched can-vas. He nodded for me to come over. A battle scene covered the canvas; a water stain darkened one corner. He flipped through a few more before looking at some of the larger paintings hanging on the walls. He pulled a few of those from their hooks and looked at the back. "You can see she's trained. Not just in how she paints, but in how she's stretched and prepped the canvases."

"She takes pride in her work," Hilda said.

"What do you think?" I whispered.

"This is big. Bigger than the Bears winning the Super Bowl. Bigger than the Cubs having a winning season." Carter bounced from foot to foot.

"Easy boy. Settle down." I looked at the canvas. "That big?" I asked.

"Bigger. People are nuts for Civil War items. These two old coots have a pile of battlefield drawings that are in great shape. Never been owned." Carter giggled. "We could sell these drawings to the right col-lector for huge green. Maybe to the *Tribune* itself."

✹

"Hilda, can you come here, sweetheart?" Carter called. "How much for these canvases?"

"These larger stretched canvases?" She thought for a second. "They're quality canvas. I'd say one hundred dollars."

"Really?" I asked.

"It's a quality base," she answered. "You can get that size with Pelican painted on it for one-fifty."

An old man with a cane had walked into the booth and looked at the canvas Carter was holding. He wore baggy, faded jeans held up by suspenders. A dirty oil company hat was on his head. "I'll take the Pelican and that sketch for three hundred," he said.

"What?" I asked.

"Five hundred," Carter countered. He tightened his grip on the sketch.

"Young man, do you know what game you're playing?" The old man coughed. "I may look like a bum, but I just bought a lake home on Lida with my Dakota oil money and I need to hang something on the walls." He planted his cane into the grass with both hands on top, looking like he wasn't going to move. "One thousand."

"There are a lot of paintings here," I offered.

"I want the Pelican and that sketch."

Carter took a step forward. "Two thousand."

I shook my head and turned to Carter. "I hope you know what you're doing," I whispered.

"Five thousand," the oilman upped it.

I bit my lip and pleaded with my eyes for Carter to let it go. But the stubborn coot was a wild dog with a piece of meat and had to show who the alpha was here.

Carter walked over to the crate with the canvases and flipped through them. "Hilda, I see twenty canvases in the crate." He slid the canvas he was holding in with the rest. "We'll take the crate and the painting for ten thousand."

"Fifteen," the oilman countered.

Carter looked at me. I shook my head and held my breath. He was playing with our entire bankroll.

"Twenty thousand for the crate of canvases and we'll leave the Pelican for our friend here."

I exhaled.

The oilman stuck out his hand and shook Carter's. "Guess I'll have to look elsewhere for the rest of my paintings." He looked at Hilda. "I'll be back for my Pelican."

Hilda pulled a receipt book and a pen from her pocket, wrote up the receipt and handed it to Carter.

Carter handed over a roll of bills from his pocket and Hilda counted them. "Grab the other end of this box, Bobby. We have some canvases to take home." He smiled and showed me the receipt written in Hilda's neat script; twenty canvases, twenty thousand dollars. At the bottom was stamped All Sales Final.

❁

Hilda handed Lois a glass of wine and toasted her with her bottle of beer. "You're a heck of an artist, my dear."

Lois steered their pontoon boat across the quiet lake. "We had a good day today. Not bad for a couple of old sisters. We're quite a team. I think we owe Bert a nice dinner. He played the oil man well."

Hilda laughed. "Ready to create some more Civil War sketches?"

About the Contributors

M.E. BAKOS has been writing fiction all of her life, and publishing short fiction since 1986. She graduated from the University of Minnesota with a B.A. in English and lives in Coon Rapids, Minnesota, with her husband, Joe Sebesta, and their spoiled dog, BonBon.

E.B. BOATNER has been a writer and photographer for nearly forty years, with stints as a histological technician, store owner, LPN, and managing editor. His articles and photos have appeared in the *Harvard University Gazette, Harvard Magazine,* and *Lavender Magazine.* He adapted his story "Satan in the Suburbs" for TV's *Monsters;* published his psychological thriller, *M-o-t-h-e-r Spells Murder,* in 2013, and wrote a play, *Changes in Time,* which premiered in the Twin Cities in 2013. Boatner lives in Minneapolis with his La-Z-Boy and is currently working on a second novel, *Who Mourns the Death of a Cabana Boy?*

CATHLENE N. BUCHHOLZ is a freelance writer and an anesthesia technician. Her writing has been featured in *Tonka Times* magazine and *Murmurs of the Past: An Anthology of Poetry and Prose.* In her spare time, she dabbles in the art of belly dance, plays guitar, and practices target shooting on her private gun range. She is currently working on two suspense novels set in the Twin Cities with her cohort in crime, William J. Anderson. Cathlene lives on a hobby farm in East Central Minnesota with her family, four dogs, two cats, and eighteen chickens.

MARLENE CHABOT lives in Fort Ripley, Minnesota, but grew up in the Twin Cities. She belongs to Great River Writers and has received a B.S. degree in education, an A.A.S. business marketing degree, and a certificate from the Institute for Children's Literature. This is her second story to be anthologized. She freelances for *Her Voice,* a *Brainerd Dispatch* quarterly magazine, has contributed to *Brainerd Dispatch* and *Central Minnesota Women* and self-published *China Connection, North Dakota Neighbor* and *Mayhem with a Capital M.* Chabot is awaiting publication of her fourth Minnesota-based mystery novel.

BARBARA MERRITT DEESE grew up in a family of voracious readers with eclectic tastes. She feels most at home with people who love a good story, which explains her love of book clubs. Deese is the author of the No Ordinary Women mysteries series, which features a book club of fun and adventurous fifty-somethings. Her twisty career path began when she became one of thirty-three female air marshals in the U.S. She lives in Minnesota with her husband and two cats.

DOUGLAS DOROW is a thriller writer living in Minneapolis, Minnesota. His first thriller, *The Ninth District*, is a Minneapolis-based FBI thriller available in paper, ebook, and audio. Currently, he's working on the second book in the series, set in Pelican Rapids, Minnesota, and a spin-off novella series featuring the FBI's Hostage Rescue Team. You can learn more about his writing and follow him on his website: www. DouglasDorow.com. On Facebook: https://www.facebook.com/DouglasDorowAuthor and on Twitter @DougDorow

D. M. S. FICK is an Emmy-nominated and PromaxBDA award winning graphic designer, animator, and illustrator. She has lived in Boston, London, and the Twin Cities. She now resides on the lone prairie in southwest Minnesota with her composer husband, some coyotes, and an occasional eagle. Ms. Fick recently finished the first book in a series featuring amateur sleuth and country music artist Lewie Sinclair, whose music is a mixture of Hank Williams and Elvis Costello. Lewie is supported on stage and off by his loyal and colorful band The Gentlemen Cowboys.

SHEYNA GALYAN is the author of the Minneapolis-based Jewish suspense series featuring Rabbi David Cohen, including *Destined to Choose* (2013) and the forthcoming *Strength to Stand* (2014). Founder and owner of award-winning Yotzeret Publishing, which specializes in books written from a Jewish perspective, Sheyna is fascinated by the intersection of tradition and technology, and her favorite questions are "Why?" and "Why not?" She holds graduate degrees in counseling psychology and education, and has worked as a counselor, consultant, lecturer, journalist, and Jewish educator. She lives with her husband, children, and a houseful of animals in St. Paul.

SUSAN HASTINGS loves stories full of suspense and can't imagine writing a story without a good dose of danger. Her first novel, *Sins of the Mother*, appeared in 2013. By day, she is the registrar at United Theological Seminary of the Twin Cities; by night, she is a graduate student at the University of St. Thomas studying international leadership. Just to make sure she's never bored, she lives in an 1884 Victorian house in St. Paul that will keep her DIY skills honed for many years to come.

CHRISTINE HUSOM is the author of the Winnebago County mystery series: *Murder in Winnebago County, Buried in Wolf Lake, An Altar by the River, The Noding Field Mystery,* and *A Death in Lionel's Woods.* She is also writing a cozy mystery series for Penguin Random House, with the first book to launch in January 2015. She holds an undergraduate degree in business and a law enforcement certificate. Husom trained with the St. Paul Police Department and served with the Wright County Sheriff's Department. She is on the Twin Cities Sisters in Crime speaker bureau panel and lives in Buffalo, Minnesota, with her family. www.christinehusom.webs.com.

MICHAEL KELBERER is a mystery writer and self-publishing enthusiast living in St. Paul, Minnesota. He was hooked on mysteries in his early teens by Dame Agatha Christie, and has read the entire Hercule Poirot series way, way more than once. He also works as a freelance business writer specializing in branding, websites, and proposals. He has three adult children. On Twitter: @MichaelKelberer and Google+: Michael Kelberer

SUSAN KOEFOD is the author of the Arvo Thorson mystery series. Her debut, *Washed Up,* was praised for its "gorgeous prose" by *Library Journal.* Other books in the series include *Broken Down* (2012) and *Burnt Out* (2013). Her poetry has been widely published, and her short story "Boys will be Boys" appeared in *Ellery Queen Mystery Magazine.* She is a recipient of a 2013 McKnight Artist Fellowship for Writers.

D.A. LAMPI was born in Fishkill, New York, and grew up in a community of Finnish immigrants with whom she danced the polka, attended a bi-weekly community sauna, and enjoyed skinny dipping afterwards in the cold waters of the Fishkill Creek. She attended New York University and The New School for Social Research where she earned her Master of Arts in psychology. Ms. Lampi lives in southeastern Minnesota. Her debut novel, *Shadow Play*, was published in June 2013. Her second novel, *An Unfortunate Death,* is planned for publication in 2014.

SHARON LEAH has worked as an editor, a patent illustrator, a floral arranger, a day care provider, and an Avon Lady. Her academic background is in art, photography, and graphic design. She has lived in Montana, Colorado, and Texas, but now calls St. Paul, Minnesota, home. This is her first published short story.

MICHAEL ALLAN MALLORY writes the Snake Jones zoo mystery series with Marilyn Victor, which features mystery's first zoologist sleuth: Lavender "Snake" Jones. *Death Roll* (2007) was praised by the *St. Paul Pioneer Press* for its "...exciting zoo setting" and "snappy, right-on dialogue." *Killer Instinct* (2011) sent Snake to the North Woods of Minnesota to encounter wolves and a murderer. *Mysterical-E* called it "...a tale that will enchant you...." Six of Michael's short stories have been published in previous anthologies. He is a member of Mystery Writers of America and is a former president of Twin Cities Sisters in Crime. www.snakejones.com.

JEANNE MULCARE's love of mysteries began in college when a friend asked her why she thought such great writers as Raymond Chandler, George Simenon, Graham Greene, and Sir Arthur Conan Doyle wrote mysteries. What possessed them? What sent them down that dark road? From that day forward Jeanne Mulcare was hooked, not just with reading mysteries and writing them, but with the dark world of crime. This is Jeanne's first published work. She lives in a suburb of St. Paul, Minnesota.

COLIN T. NELSON became hooked on mystery stories when he spent Christmas vacations with his grandmother. She gave him a copy of *The Hound of the Baskervilles* which inspired him to write mysteries. In the meantime, he worked for more than thirty years as both a prosecutor and a public defender. He has published three suspense mysteries: *Reprisal,*

Fallout, and *Flashover.* He is married and has two adult children. When he has time, Colin plays the saxophone and flute in a jazz group called *Blue Mood.*

MICKIE TURK has worked independently and commercially in film, photography, and journalism for the past twenty years. She wrote, directed, and produced films—both short and feature-length narratives and documentaries. Her travels to Cuba produced a film on the religion Santeria and *Havana Nights,* a locally screened shorts film festival. Early educational and employment experiences included adult mental health services and juvenile community corrections. Mickie has written novels, screenplays, and a variety of short stories and memoirs. Most recently, she is film curator at Edina Film Festival and vice president of Twin Cities Chapter of Sisters In Crime. http://mickieturkauthor.blogspot.com

CHERYL ULLYOT retired from Northwest Airlines in 2008 after 39 years of service as a flight attendant. An avid mystery reader, she has turned to mystery writing in her retirement. She is a member of Mystery Writers of America, Sisters in Crime, and a supportive writing group. She has written articles for local publications in the Twin Cities, and is currently working on her first novel, an airline murder mystery. The Looney Daze story was inspired by her visit to Vergas, Minnesota, while vacationing in the Brainerd area during the summer of 2013.